"Peter, can you say the blessing for the food?" Amelia's father asked.

"Okay," Peter said. Bowing his head, Peter wished his boss had asked his missionary daughter to say the prayer. Wasn't she better equipped for such a duty? Was it right to ask God to help you say a prayer? he wondered. Because that's what he planned to do.

Peter closed his eyes. He said the blessing, which included the Lord bringing Amelia home safely, then glanced at Amelia.

"Thank you for the prayer," she said. "I appreciate your mentioning all the dear friends I had to leave. I wish I could have brought them home with me." She smiled at him, while her eyes welled with tears again.

Peter had that strange urge once more to pull her into his embrace and comfort her.

Books by Merrillee Whren

Love Inspired

The Heart's Homecoming
An Unexpected Blessing
Love Walked In
The Heart's Forgiveness
Four Little Blessings
Mommy's Hometown Hero
Homecoming Blessings

MERRILLEE WHREN

is the winner of the 2003 Golden Heart Award for best inspirational romance manuscript presented by Romance Writers of America. In 2004, she made her first sale to Steeple Hill Books. She is married to her own personal hero, her husband of thirty-plus years, and has two grown daughters. She has lived in Atlanta, Boston, Dallas and Chicago but now makes her home on one of God's most beautiful creations, an island off the east coast of Florida. When she's not writing or working for her husband's recruiting firm, she spends her free time playing tennis or walking the beach, where she does the plotting for her novels. Please visit her Web site at www.merrilleewhren.com.

Homecoming Blessings
Merrillee Whren

Steeple
Hill®

Published by Steeple Hill Books™

STEEPLE HILL BOOKS

Steeple
Hill®

Recycling programs
for this product may
not exist in your area.

ISBN-13: 978-0-373-87525-2
ISBN-10:   0-373-87525-8

HOMECOMING BLESSINGS

www.SteepleHill.com

Printed in U.S.A.

What good is it, my brothers, if a man claims to have faith but has no deeds? Can such faith save him? Suppose a brother or sister is without clothes and daily food. If one of you says to him, Go, I wish you well, keep warm and well fed, but does nothing about his physical needs, what good is it? In the same way, faith by itself, if it is not accompanied by action, is dead. But someone will say, You have faith, I have deeds. Show me your faith without deeds, and I will show you my faith by what I do.

—*James* 2:14–18

Since this is the last book in the series about the
Dalton brothers, Wade, Matt and Peter,
I want to dedicate this book to my three brothers,
Greg, Gary and George.

I want to give special thanks to my friends
Lynn and Jim Soltys who graciously opened
their home for my visit and research trip to the
North Georgia mountains.

Chapter One

Broken glass, glittering in the warm April sun, covered the sidewalk outside a storefront in the nearly completed strip mall. A white truck with blue lettering on the side that read "Do It Yourself Movers" sat half in and half out of one of the windows. Taking in the mess, Peter Dalton carefully pocketed his cell phone in a conscious effort to keep himself from slinging it across the parking lot.

Rubbing the back of his neck, he approached the police car where two uniformed officers questioned a young man about the runaway truck. Before Peter reached them, his cell phone rang. *Now what?* He yanked the phone from his pocket and looked at the caller ID. His boss, Richard Hiatt of Hiatt Construction, wasn't going to be happy about this.

Perspiration trickling down his back, Peter flipped open the phone. "Hello, Richard. I suppose you've heard about the accident at the Carson Corners project."

"Yes, something about a truck."

"Smashed right through the front window of one of the units. The police are investigating now."

"I'm sure they'll get to the bottom of it."

"I'm checking into it."

"Don't bother. I'm sending Mark Becker over there to deal with it. He's on his way. I've got something more important for you to do."

"What's that?"

"I'm up here in Alpharetta, and the traffic on Georgia 400 is stopped dead because of an accident. I'm supposed to be at the airport to meet Ashley in less than an hour. Even if traffic clears, I'm not going to make it. I want you to pick her up."

Peter gripped the phone. Taking care of the boss's daughter was the last thing he wanted to do, but Peter's primary goal in life was pleasing his boss. "Isn't Mark closer to the airport?"

"Yes, but Mark's a stranger. She knows you."

"Barely. Are you sure she remembers me?"

"At least you'll be a familiar face. She's never met Mark." The concern was evident in Richard's voice. "I feel terrible. Here she is, coming back after five years away from home, and I can't be there."

"Don't worry. I'll take care of it." With guilt nipping at his heels, Peter strode toward his silver SUV. Uneasiness replaced the guilt as he slipped behind the wheel. Richard Hiatt had mentored him through the construction business, and Peter didn't want to take one step that would jeopardize their relationship or his rising opportunities with Hiatt Construction. "Does she have a cell phone?"

"No cell phone. No need for one of those in the African countryside. Besides, after the unrest started, she barely escaped with a few belongings."

"That's too bad."

"I'm just grateful that she's fine."

"How's she going to know I'm picking her up instead of you?" Peter wondered whether he would recognize the girl he'd met on brief occasions in the years he'd worked for Hiatt.

"You can make a sign with her name on it."

"Okay, and I need her flight info."

"I'll have my assistant text you the information."

"I'm on my way." Peter started the car.

"Oh, and Peter, when you bring Ashley home, I want you to stay for dinner. We have some things to discuss."

What could his boss possibly want to talk about? Surely the man wouldn't want to discuss business when his daughter had just returned. Impressions of Richard and his daughter, Ashley, raced through his head like the cars zooming down the interstate. Over the years, Peter had heard Richard say that he and Ashley didn't agree on much. What was the state of their father-daughter relationship now? Before today, his boss hadn't mentioned that she was coming home, much less that unrest in the country where she served as a missionary and teacher had precipitated the return.

Had Ashley changed in five years? He had a vague memory of a tall, thin girl with an unruly mane of honey-colored hair and light brown eyes hidden behind owlish glasses that were always slipping down her freckled nose. She'd been just out of college when she left to serve in the mission field.

The questions flitted through Peter's mind as he passed by Georgia Tech and The Varsity, Atlanta's famous drive-in hamburger joint. The skyscrapers of downtown Atlanta loomed ahead, and he forced himself to pay attention to the traffic, as a sea of red taillights spelled trouble. Stepping on the brake, he glanced at the clock on the dash. Ten minutes to one. Not only was Richard unable to be at the airport to meet his daughter, but it appeared that his stand-in wouldn't be there to greet her, either.

Barely able to keep her eyes open, Ashley clung to the pole in the train as the automated voice announced the departure to the next concourse. Catnaps on what seemed like never-ending plane rides hadn't been much help over the past twenty-four hours. When the voice declared their arrival at baggage claim, she joined the crowd that surged out of the train and jostled to get on the escalators. Her backpack felt as though it weighed a ton.

When she stepped off the escalator, she glanced around the area, searching for her father. A large man with thick gray hair, he was easily identifiable, even in a crowd, but she didn't see him. A sinking sensation hit her stomach when she spied the handsome man with sandy-brown hair, clutching a makeshift sign with "Ashley Hiatt" written on it in bold, black letters. He looked just the same as the last time she'd seen him. Even his navy-blue blazer and khaki pants with the sharp creases hadn't changed a bit.

Why was Peter Dalton here instead of her father? Ashley tried to smile, but it was hard to do, knowing her father couldn't be bothered to come to the airport to greet her. After five years how could he ignore the arrival of his only child?

Even the man her father had sent to get her was looking past her as if she was invisible. She'd never been the type to attract the attention of a man like Peter. Growing up, she'd seen him numerous times at church or at her father's social gatherings. He always had a beautiful woman on his arm.

Adjusting her backpack, she maneuvered her way through the crowd. But before she reached Peter, he glanced her way. His gaze held hers, and he smiled. She stopped. Her pulse raced, a completely unexpected reaction. She swallowed a lump in her throat as he continued toward her. Taking a deep breath, she gave him a little wave.

"Ashley." His smile broadened into a grin. "I was afraid I wasn't going to get here on time or find you when I did."

"Well, you did." He remembered her. Why did that please her? She pushed the question to the back of her mind.

"Your dad sent me to get you because—"

"I can see that." Not wanting to hear her father's excuses, she cut Peter off.

"Do you have luggage?"

"Just the backpack."

"Would you like me to carry it for you?"

"Sure. It's getting heavy." Ashley shrugged out of the pack and handed it to him.

Their fingers brushed, and her pulse jumped again. Why was she having heart palpitations over Peter Dalton? Her reaction must be due to lack of sleep and the adrenaline rush that had come from her hurried departure from the place she'd called home for the last five years.

He lifted the backpack onto his shoulder. "Wow! You have rocks in here?"

Ashley laughed as they made their way toward the exit. "No. A few clothes and some books, but I was beginning to feel like it was filled with rocks, too."

Hazel eyes twinkling, he laughed in return. "My car's this way. Follow me."

Ashley fell into step beside him as they walked toward the parking lot. "I suppose my dad was too busy working to—"

"Actually, he's stuck in traffic up in Alpharetta. Some big accident on 400. He felt pretty awful about not being able to meet you."

"Stuck in traffic," Ashley repeated, barely above a whisper, and wondered if that was really true. She hated doubting her father's word, but he'd always been good at making excuses for missing important events in her life. After her mother died, her father had never been quite the same fun-loving man. He let work take over his life.

"Yeah. You can use my cell to call him if you'd like." Peter unlocked his SUV and opened the passenger door.

"Thanks." She climbed in and settled on the leather seat.

He held up the backpack. "Do you want this, or should I put it in the backseat?"

She reached for it. "I'll take it."

Their fingers brushed again. She steeled herself against her earlier reaction, but her pulse raced again. Taking a deep breath, she closed her eyes.

"Tired?"

"A little." Opening her eyes, she straightened in the seat and glanced at Peter.

He held out his phone to her. "His number's already up. Push the green button."

"Thanks." Ashley listened to the ringtone as they merged onto the highway.

Her father's voice came over the phone. "Peter, you got my baby?"

"Daddy, it's me. I'm using Peter's cell. And I'm not your baby."

Her father's big, booming laugh sounded in her ear. "Ashley, sugar, you'll always be my baby as long as I live. So sorry I didn't make it to the airport. This Atlanta traffic gets worse every year."

"That's okay, Daddy."

"No, it's not okay, but I'll make it up to you when you get home. I can hardly wait to see my baby girl." He laughed again. "This traffic still isn't moving. You'll probably beat me home."

"I'll be glad to see you, too," Ashley said, feeling much better. She should forget the past. This was a chance to have a new start.

"Remind Peter that I want him to stay for dinner, and have him stop so you can buy a few clothes."

"He probably doesn't have time for that."

"Sure he does. You have to have something to wear until your things arrive from overseas."

"Okay. I'll see you in a little bit. 'Bye." Ashley flipped the phone closed. "Daddy said to remind you that you're supposed to stay for dinner."

Peter kept his focus on the road. "What else did he say?"

Lying wasn't an option, but she was tempted. If Peter was like most guys, he probably wanted to take her shopping about as much as he wanted his feet set on fire.

She let out a sigh. "He said to stop so I can buy some clothes. I had to ship most of my stuff. With our rushed departure, I'm not sure if it'll ever get here."

"That's tough, but there's no problem stopping. Where do you want to shop? Perimeter Mall?"

"Just take me to that discount store on Abernathy."

"Gotcha."

Ashley studied him as he concentrated on his driving. He said he didn't mind stopping, but did she detect irritation in his voice? Sometimes her father could be overbearing, but she thought she remembered Peter as a man who wasn't intimidated by her father's authoritative style. Yet Peter always seemed to do whatever her father asked.

But why, on her homecoming, had her father insisted they share dinner with a business associate? Wouldn't it be better to have a private family reunion? Would they spend the time discussing business? She hoped not. She couldn't figure out her father. Never could, probably never would.

"How does it feel to be back home?" Peter gave her a sideways glance.

"To be honest, I haven't considered Atlanta home in a long time. I'm used to a simple life without a lot of the things people here take for granted—like air conditioning, TV and cell phones."

"I had no idea your conditions were so primitive."

"Primitive?" Ashley stifled a laugh. "Oh, I hardly call living without those things primitive. The missionaries had a very nice residence. But primitive conditions exist in some of the villages, where the people still live in grass huts. They have very few possessions. They taught me that material things aren't the important things in life. You should hear them sing praises to God. Their voices are marvelous."

"Your father said something about unrest in the country. What happened?"

Ashley closed her eyes and pressed her hand to her mouth in an effort to control her emotions.

"You don't want to talk about it?"

Shaking her head, Ashley looked at Peter. Concern wrinkled his handsome brow. He seemed to understand her reaction, and she was surprised. She'd never had a very positive view of this man. He always seemed interested only in money and beautiful women. In her opinion, "shallow" described him perfectly. But maybe he wasn't shallow after all. "You can't imagine what it was like. I already miss the people there so much. I know they're in God's hands, but it was hard to leave them. I've been praying constantly that they'll be safe."

"It was bad?"

Ashley nodded. "Daddy will want a report, so I'll explain everything at dinner. I don't think I can relive it twice."

"Sure."

"All I've ever wanted to do is serve God. Now I'm wondering what God wants for my life?" Leaving the mission field hadn't been in her plans. She hoped the bitterness in her heart didn't come across in her words.

"Maybe God wants you home with your father."

Why would God want that? The question sat on the tip of her tongue, but she bit her bottom lip in order not to ask it. Peter couldn't be right. Her father didn't need her. He had everything money could buy.

Peter took the exit for Abernathy Road off of State Road 400.

"Are you sure you only want to go to the discount store? The mall's just down this road the other way."

"The discount store will be quicker."

"Whatever you say."

"I hate that you have to do this."

"I don't mind. I can pick up a few things myself."

As he turned into the parking lot and found a parking space near the main entrance, she wondered whether he really had shopping to do. Maybe he was just being polite. She hated feeling like a burden.

"I won't be long," she said as they entered the store.

"Take your time." He motioned toward the women's clothing section straight ahead. "I'll meet you right over there when I'm finished."

"You think you'll be finished before I am?"

He chuckled. "I've never known a woman who could pick out clothes in the time it'll take me to throw a few items into a cart."

"Then you don't know me."

Grinning, he shook his head. "You're right, but I still don't think you can pick out your clothes faster than I can get the things I need."

"We'll see about that." She grabbed a cart and hurried off while he went in the opposite direction. The grin he'd given her when he left was almost a smirk. He thought he knew so much about women. Well, he didn't know about this woman. She'd show him that it didn't take her forever to shop for clothes.

Speed was the most important part of this shopping trip. Hoping Peter wouldn't notice them when they checked out, Ashley plucked three packages of ladies' briefs off the shelf and threw them in the cart, then added other items she needed, along with a comfortable-looking pajama set.

Next stop: sportswear. Feeling like one of those contestants in a shopping spree show, she wheeled her cart through the aisle, almost running into another shopper. She whipped through the rack of twill pants and selected two pairs, in khaki and black, then two pairs of cropped pants, one navy blue and the other white. She scurried over to a tiered table with a display of knit tops and grabbed four in various colors.

Casting a glance over her shoulder, she strode into the dress section. No sign of Peter. That was good. She rifled through the sale rack and found a little black dress and a red shirtdress in her size and dumped them in the cart. As she sped toward the checkout, she noticed the shoes. Did she need shoes? She glanced at her comfortable, clunky sandals. They would have to do for now. Time was more important than shoes. She could get those later. Peter wasn't going to win, even if she had to go barefoot.

While she contemplated her need for shoes, Peter came down the aisle. He pushed a nearly empty cart. The surprise on his face was priceless and worth going without shoes.

He stopped beside her. "You're done?"

"Yes. How about you?" She fought the smile threatening to curve her lips. "I said you wouldn't have to wait."

Glancing at her cart, he chuckled halfheartedly. "Did you try any of that stuff on?"

"No."

"Are you sure that's wise?"

"It'll be fine." She maneuvered her cart into the checkout lane. When he went into another lane, she breathed a sigh of relief.

"Who gave you the lessons in speed shopping?" he asked as they exited the store.

"My dad."

Laughing out loud, he unlocked the car. "That explains it."

"Why? Have you been shopping with Daddy?"

"Not for clothes, but I went with him once when he was shopping for tools. He was in and out of the store before I'd found a place to park."

"I come by it naturally then. Leisurely shopping isn't in our genes."

"I'll remember that the next time I take you shopping."

Yeah. Like there would be a next time. To her surprise, this little excursion had been kind of fun. The thought of there being a next time gave her a slight thrill of pleasure. She shook her head to clear her thoughts, unsure as to why Peter was making such an impression on her today.

Minutes later, Peter turned his SUV off Roswell Road. A sense of anticipation unsettled her as they entered the subdivision surrounding the golf course where her father played every weekend. When Peter drove up the street leading to her childhood home, a lump formed in Ashley's throat, while a strange pressure filled her chest.

Birch and pine trees surrounded the two-story, tan brick house that sat on a hillside covered with English ivy. White dogwoods dressed the yard in lace. A lump rose in her throat when she saw the welcoming warmth of the red front door. She never expected this reaction to seeing the house again.

"Well, we're here. Whose car is in the driveway?"

Ashley shrugged. "It doesn't belong to my dad?"

"I don't recognize it." Peter hurried around the front of the vehicle as Ashley got out. "When you talked with him, did he say anyone would be at the house?"

"No. He only told me we'd probably beat him here." Adjusting the backpack on her shoulder, she grabbed the bags of clothing from the backseat.

"Do you need help with your stuff?"

She looked up at him, and noticed again how handsome he was. She smiled and shook her head. "No, thanks. I've got it." She lowered her gaze and turned toward the front door wondering again who she would find on the other side.

Chapter Two

Stopping in the middle of the walk, Peter watched Ashley head for the door. A smile tugged at the corners of his mouth. The strong-willed young woman who'd defied her father and gone to the mission field had lost none of her feistiness. Their shopping trip proved that.

Before she reached the porch, the front door flew open. Ashley stopped short and let her backpack and shopping bags fall to the walk. "Charlotte, what are you doing here?"

With arms spread wide, Richard Hiatt's housekeeper raced down the front steps. "Ashley, you're here. Your daddy called and asked me to open up the house and fix dinner." The older woman gathered Ashley into her arms. "It's so good to have you home."

He'd rarely seen Charlotte Perdue since Ashley had gone away, although she cleaned house for Richard a couple of times a week. Peter marveled that the woman hardly seemed to have aged, except for a sprinkling of gray in her dark-brown hair.

The two women stepped onto the porch, then stopped. Charlotte turned and motioned toward him. "Well, don't just stand there, Peter. Come inside."

"Yes, ma'am." He jogged toward the porch and scooped up

Ashley's bags and backpack as he went by. He joined Ashley and Charlotte in the two-story foyer and set the backpack and bags next to the stairway.

Looking around, Ashley placed a hand over her heart. "Everything's changed. When did Daddy redecorate?"

"Last year. Do you like it?"

Ashley hesitated, then slowly pivoted in a complete circle, taking in the Oriental rugs and golden hardwood floors that adorned the living room and dining room on either side of the foyer. "It's lovely, but I liked the old stuff."

"That was the problem. It was old—some of it from before you were born."

"But that's just it. Those things spelled home to me and gave me pleasant memories of my mother. Now they're gone."

"I didn't know you were so attached to those old things." Charlotte patted Ashley on the shoulder.

Ashley bit her lower lip, then sighed. "Neither did I."

Taking in the exchange, Peter recognized the surprise in Ashley's voice as she admitted her love for the things her father had discarded. With her flowing ankle-length print skirt, short-sleeved knit top and sturdy sandals, along with the speed shopping, he would have thought she wasn't interested in fashion or the latest in home furnishings.

As she started toward the short hallway leading to the back of the house, he picked up her things. "Here's your stuff. What should I do with it?"

She stared at him for a moment, amber eyes sparkling in the sunlight that streamed through the large arched window above the front door. Were those unshed tears about her mother's stuff? Her mother had been gone for nearly twenty years, and Ashley had been away from home for five. Why did it bother her now?

For a split second he was tempted to gather her in his arms and tell her everything would be all right. But it wasn't his place. Surprised by his own reaction, he stepped back and gripped the strap on her backpack as if it were a lifeline to save him from his crazy thoughts.

Before Ashley could answer, Charlotte stepped between them. "I'll take the bags."

Ashley extended her hand. "And I'll take the backpack."

He gave it to her, careful not to make contact. When their fingers had brushed earlier in the car, something about her touch made him jumpy. He'd forgotten for a moment that she was the boss's daughter.

She slung the backpack over her shoulder and headed toward the kitchen at the back of the house. "I need to put these dirty clothes in the laundry room."

"Of course." Charlotte went ahead of Ashley into the kitchen. "I'll just put these bags by the back stairs. You remember where the laundry room is?"

"Sure. Daddy didn't rearrange the rooms, too, did he?"

The two women laughed over Ashley's remark. Peter couldn't help watching her. She'd always been thin, but she appeared waif-like now, her clothes hanging on her slender frame. Although she'd replaced her owlish glasses with a more stylish pair, they still had a tendency to slip down her freckled nose. Wisps of her seemingly untamable hair had escaped from the elastic holding it back from her face.

She painted a picture of vulnerability. But that's not how he remembered her, or how she'd been today until she'd seen the changes in this house. Strong. Opinionated. Those words portrayed the young woman he'd known before she went to the mission field as a teacher. Was she still the same, or had the time away changed her?

When she walked into the kitchen, Ashley stopped, much the same as she had when she'd first walked into the house. She gazed around the room at the cherry cabinets and granite countertops. "Everything's new in here, too." A hint of sadness colored her words. "Daddy never told me. This doesn't even look like the same house inside."

"You'll get used to it." Charlotte hurried across the kitchen and deposited the bags by the stairs, then opened the door to the laundry room. "Put your things in here, and I'll take care of them."

"Thanks." Ashley unzipped the backpack, withdrew a bundle of clothing and threw it into a laundry basket. Coming back into the kitchen, she looked at Charlotte. "What about my room? Will I recognize it, or did Daddy change everything in there, too?"

"He hasn't changed a thing." Charlotte smiled.

Ashley sighed. "That's a relief. I shouldn't be upset, I know. I think I was just shocked because I didn't know it would be different."

"Your reaction is completely understandable." Charlotte patted Ashley on the shoulder again. "But one thing hasn't changed. Your favorite meal. At least I hope it's still your favorite."

"Lasagna?"

"Yes. I've got it ready to put in the oven as soon as we hear from your father."

"Do you suppose I have time to take a shower before he gets home? I feel so grungy after the long flight."

"I don't know. Call him." Charlotte handed the phone to Ashley. "His number's on speed dial. Number one."

"What other number could he be?" Ashley laughed as she punched in the number. After a short conversation, she hung up and turned to Charlotte. "He says traffic's just starting to move. He figures it'll be at least a half hour, maybe more, before he gets here."

Charlotte opened the refrigerator. "That gives you time to take a quick shower, and I'll pop this lasagna into the oven. It should be ready when he walks in the door."

"We wouldn't want to keep him waiting." Ashley started for

the back stairs, then stopped. She turned and looked at Peter. "I'm sorry. I didn't mean to run off and leave you."

"No problem. Charlotte and I will have a good talk while you're gone." He winked at Charlotte. "We have lots to catch up on."

"But you're catching up without me." Ashley picked up the bags sitting next to the stairs.

Peter chuckled. "Believe me. We'll save the good stuff till you get back."

"Okay, I'll hold you to that."

As she headed up the stairs, Peter marveled at how much he was enjoying Ashley's company.

"Ashley hasn't changed much, has she?" Charlotte's comment interrupted Peter's musings.

He turned her way. How could he answer the question? Ashley's disagreements with her father were about the only thing he remembered. "I didn't know her very well. She was just twelve when I came to work for her father after college. I saw her off and on through the years, but never really got to know her. Then she went away to college and off to the mission field."

Charlotte nodded. "Yes, I guess you weren't around her much. Sometimes I feel as though I didn't know her that well myself."

"I always got the impression she liked to march to the beat of her own drum, especially where her father was concerned."

"You've got that right." Charlotte chuckled. "Those two didn't agree on much once Ashley became a teenager, and the disagreements continued right up until she left home."

"Do you think she knows we're talking about her now that she's gone?" Peter poured himself some iced tea from the pitcher sitting on the counter.

Charlotte smiled wryly. "Probably."

Peter wondered how Ashley's return would affect his boss. "Do you think they'll get along better now?"

"Good question. I didn't think it was my place to interfere while Ashley was growing up, but there were times when I thought Mr. Hiatt indulged that girl too much. He made his own monster, and then he had to live with it."

"Ashley, the monster." Peter grinned at the thought. He couldn't help noticing after all of these years that Charlotte still referred to Richard as "Mr. Hiatt."

"Maybe I've spoken out of turn." Charlotte got a bowl from the cupboard and started making a salad. "I wish I'd been able to mother her a little, but she never let anyone get very close after her mother died. She spent most of her time in her room with a book. That child certainly loved to read."

"Reading's a good thing," he said, remembering how he'd spent hours and hours reading as a kid when he wasn't playing some kind of sport with his brothers. Maybe that was the difference. Ashley never had siblings to coax her away from the books.

"Oh, I have no doubt reading was a good pastime for her, but she seemed to use reading to avoid any interest in 'girl' things like makeup, hair or boys. One time, I tried to talk her into going to a party with a neighbor boy."

"And?"

"And Mr. Hiatt let me know Ashley would make up her own mind." Charlotte continued working without looking his way. "I think sometimes he wasn't sure how to deal with her growing up. He didn't want to admit she wasn't a kid anymore, even when she went away to college."

"So you're saying he told you to mind your own business?"

"Not in those words, but I got the message." Charlotte shrugged, frowning a little. "That's why I said he made his own monster. He let her make her own decisions about everything."

"Everything?"

"Well, not everything, but he encouraged her to be her own person and speak her own mind. So one day she decided to go on a mission. There was no talking her out of it. He'd given her free rein, and he couldn't pull her back in."

"What do you suppose he'll do now that she's back? While we were talking on the drive from the airport, I got the feeling that Ashley's at a crossroads and doesn't know what to do."

"That's understandable. Her whole life's been turned upside down." Charlotte set the salad bowl aside. "I don't know what her father intends to do, but I'm going to try to fatten her up a little while she's home. She's gotten way too thin."

Although he'd made the same observation, Peter thought it better not to comment. He walked over to the bay windows that looked out on the terraced back yard and patio surrounded by stately oak, maple and birch trees. "I wonder whether her ears are burning? Maybe we ought to change the subject."

"Okay," Charlotte said. "Let's talk about you. What's been happening in your life? Are you seeing a special lady?"

"No one special." Now that was a subject Peter *didn't* want to discuss. He never lacked for female companionship when he wanted it, but he avoided serious relationships. The breakup of his engagement right after college had had a lasting effect on him. He never wanted to hurt like that again. Whenever he sensed a woman was becoming too interested, he broke off the relationship. He should've overcome his fear of being hurt by now, but he hadn't yet met a woman who was worth the risk of another broken heart.

"What's wrong with you young people today? I guess you're all too busy for relationships."

"Probably." Peter wasn't about to argue and wondered how this woman who'd been a widow for a half-dozen years could fault him for not having a serious romantic relationship.

"Maybe you and Ashley would make a good match."

Peter nearly spewed a mouthful of iced tea all over the kitchen. Now that was laughable. The sweet missionary girl wouldn't find much to like in him. Sure, he attended church, but his dedication was suspect. And his goal in life lay far, far away from mission work. He liked working hard and making money—and one day hopefully he would be the boss of Hiatt Construction. "Uh, she wouldn't be interested in me."

Charlotte opened the oven and placed a baking sheet full of garlic bread on the rack. Closing the oven door, she looked up at Peter. "You could always work on changing that. You men like a challenge, don't you?"

Peter went over and draped an arm around Charlotte's shoulders. "You may be right about men liking a challenge, but Ashley Hiatt is one I don't want to tackle. So put those matchmaking thoughts right back where they came from."

Charlotte let out a loud chuckle, then gave him a laser-beam look that reminded him of his mother. "You might be surprised at what you can tackle."

"Not me." Shaking his head, he pointed to himself. "I'm a wimp when it comes to women."

Ashley stared at her reflection. The red top and khaki pants she'd purchased this afternoon hung on her. Nothing fit, except the black dress. She should've tried everything on, but she'd wanted to prove to Peter that he was wrong to lump her in with a bunch of women who spent too much time on their clothes, hair and makeup. Much to her chagrin, she was worried about her clothes anyway. She had proved nothing.

How was she going to face him in these pants that made her look like a clown? She had no choice but to deal with the consequences of her misguided actions.

Stopping for a moment, she bowed her head. *Lord, forgive me for being prideful and thinking only of myself.* She took a deep breath and fluffed her damp curls with her fingers as she headed for the stairs. That was the wonderful thing about God. He was there to forgive and pick her up when she stumbled.

Besides, she shouldn't be thinking about Peter. He probably wouldn't notice her clothes anyway. He was only concerned about doing her father's bidding. As she neared the last step, she heard Peter's voice over the sound of Charlotte's laughter.

"Ask anyone who knows me," Peter said as Ashley stepped into the kitchen.

"Y'all are having too much fun without me," she said brightly.

Peter whirled around and waved a hand at Charlotte. "Charlotte and I were just kidding with each other."

"I could hear you laughing." Ashley shoved at her glasses and looked at Peter. Sporting an uncertain smile, he appeared to be worried that she'd been eavesdropping. Had they been talking about her?

"We'll have a better time now that you're here," Charlotte said as the buzzer on the oven went off. She hurried over and took the bread out of the oven and placed it in an oblong breadbasket. The smell of garlic wafted through the kitchen.

Ashley glanced at Peter, who lounged against the doorframe near the windows. She didn't miss the way he crossed his arms and continued to look slightly guilty about something. Or was he looking at her ill-fitting clothes? "Somehow I think I've already missed the fun."

Shaking her head, Charlotte pulled plates and glasses from the cupboard and set them on the counter. "You didn't miss much. I was just giving Peter a hard time about his lack of a love life."

Ashley raised her eyebrows as she looked at him. "*You* have no love life? What happened to all the women who used to hang around you? Every time I saw you, you were with a different beautiful girl. You had to shoo them away like flies."

Laughing, Charlotte got navy-blue cloth napkins and placemats out of a drawer and set them next to the plates. "That's why he doesn't have a serious girlfriend. He's run them all off."

Peter looked as though he wanted to dump the pan of caramelized walnuts that Charlotte was preparing right on her head instead of in the salad. "Don't pay any attention to her. She's just trying to make me feel bad because I haven't settled down yet. But I kind of like my bachelor life."

"That's what all these men say, but they don't mean it." Charlotte winked at Ashley, then motioned toward the plates. "You two can set the table in the dining room. I'm thinking Mr. Hiatt will want to eat in there to celebrate Ashley's homecoming."

. Without a word, Peter grabbed the plates, placemats and napkins and charged toward the dining room. Was he trying to get away from the issue of his nonexistent love life? Was he no longer Atlanta's most eligible bachelor, with a dozen pretty women clamoring for his attention? Ashley opened a nearby drawer and gathered flatware, then headed for the dining room.

When she entered the room, she expected to see a grumpy Peter slapping placemats and plates on the table. Instead, the plates, placemats and napkins sat on one end of the table while he lounged against the doorframe at the other end of the room. As he looked her over from head to toe, an I-told-you-so grin split his handsome face. He didn't have to say a word. She knew exactly what he was thinking.

Looking directly at him, she squared her shoulders. "All right. So I should've tried on the clothes."

"Did I say anything about your clothes?" He pushed away from the doorframe and walked toward her.

"You didn't have to. Your smirk said it all." Glancing down, she pulled out the sides of the oversized pants. "They're too big."

"You think?"

"Don't rub it in."

"I won't. I think you're kinda cute in your oversized bloomers."

Warmth crept up her neck. She hoped her cheeks weren't turning pink. "You said you weren't going to rub it in, but now you're teasing me."

"I'm not teasing you. I'm giving you a compliment."

"Well, I can do without your compliments, thank you."

Before Ashley could say anything else, her father burst into the room.

"Daddy!" She ran and threw her arms around him.

He gave her a big bear hug, then held her at arm's length. "It's so good to see you." He hugged her again.

"Dad, you're squishing me."

"Sorry, sugar. I just missed you so much. I can hardly believe you're finally home." He looked up at Peter. "Thanks for fetching her for me."

"My pleasure."

Wondering whether Peter's words rang true, she picked up the placemats and arranged them on the table. Peter quickly followed her lead, taking the plates and putting them on the placemats.

"Do these women have you setting the table?"

Peter nodded and looked up at Richard. "Yes, sir. That's my pleasure, too. Did you hear anything more about the runaway truck?"

"Yes, seems the young man had rented the truck to move his furniture and parked it up the street to unload it. The parking brake didn't hold on the hill, and the thing rolled down and crashed into our building."

Despite her curiosity, Ashley didn't want to engage in business talk. That was one aspect of her father's life she wanted to avoid. Now that she was back, she feared he would try to get her involved in the construction business as he'd tried to do before she went to the mission field.

Ashley turned toward the kitchen. "We don't have any glasses on the table. I'll get them."

"Good. That'll give me a moment to fill Peter in on the accident," Richard said.

Ashley stopped in the doorway and glanced back. "What do you want to drink?"

"Iced tea for me. No sugar." Richard patted his stomach. "Got to watch those calories these days."

Peter nodded. "Make mine the same."

"Sure." Ashley scurried into the kitchen.

For a few minutes she'd almost liked Peter, but now she remembered why he irritated her on so many levels. He was always trying to please her father, no matter what the request. His kindness to her was all part of the plan to please his boss. Even before she'd left the room, he was completely involved in business talk with her dad.

Setting the four glasses on the counter, Ashley realized she was judging Peter pretty harshly. God loved Peter. He was here at her father's request, and he'd helped today. So she should get over her own prejudices. Peter and her father had business to talk about. Just because she didn't care for the business world didn't mean that others shouldn't.

Doing the right thing still didn't always come easily, even though she'd been a missionary for five years and sometimes felt she should have that whole "loving your neighbor as yourself" conquered by now. Her attitude toward Peter clearly showed that she didn't. While she filled the glasses with iced tea, she asked God for forgiveness again.

She glanced over at Charlotte, who was putting the dressing on the salad. "What would you like to drink?"

"Water for me."

After pouring the water, Ashley put the glasses on a tray and took them to the dining room. When she entered the room, Peter immediately came toward her. "Let me help you with that."

"Sure." She looked up at him, and her heart jumped just as it had when she'd seen him at the airport. She took a deep breath. Her reaction must be the result of jet lag.

Chapter Three

Thoughts of Ashley tumbled through Peter's mind as he returned to the kitchen with her. Why did it bother him that she remembered his girlfriends? Ever since coming to work for Hiatt Construction, he'd changed girlfriends as often as he'd changed the oil in his car. Did that make her think he couldn't hang on to a woman?

"The table's set. Do we need to do anything else?" Ashley asked Charlotte.

"No. Everything's ready. This has to sit for a few minutes before I cut it." Charlotte took the lasagna out of the oven and set the steaming casserole dish on the nearby cooktop.

"It sure smells good." Richard plucked a walnut from the top of the salad. "I'm glad you decided to eat in the dining room. This is a celebration."

"Stop picking at the food before it's on the table." Charlotte swatted at his hand.

Winking, Richard pulled his hand back. "Yes, ma'am."

Peter took in their playful actions. After all of these years, was something going on between his boss and the housekeeper?

Richard had been a widower for nearly twenty years. Could

it be that he was suddenly finding romance with Charlotte? Peter dismissed the idea. He was probably reading way more into their behavior than he should. After all, she still called him Mr. Hiatt. Peter had observed the times friends and coworkers tried to fix his boss up with someone. Richard would have nothing to do with it. The man had always seemed satisfied with his single life.

Peter liked the single life, too. At thirty-eight, he still had no desire to get married. Most relationships weren't worth the time and bother. Over fifteen years had passed since his fiancée had crushed his heart with her betrayal, yet he still didn't feel like setting himself up for another heartache.

"Chocolate cake? How am I going to resist? You're making it hard for me to stay on my diet." Richard's voice shook Peter from his thoughts.

"Chocolate cake sounds good to me," Peter agreed.

Charlotte began cutting the lasagna in to neat squares. "Mr. H, the cake's for Ashley's homecoming. It's her favorite. I've fixed all of her favorites."

"One tiny piece won't hurt you, Daddy." Ashley sidled up beside her father and put her arm through his.

Richard patted his daughter's hand and laughed. "You two are going to make me fat, and you don't even care."

"Oh, but I do care. I'll cut a very tiny piece for you." Ashley gave her father an impish grin.

"Okay, we're set." Using a pair of oven mitts, Charlotte placed the casserole containing the lasagna into a silver server, and held it out to Richard. "You can take this into the dining room and set it on the table, but be careful not to burn yourself. It's really hot."

Shaking his head, Richard picked up the lasagna. "You'd think I was a little kid the way she talks to me. I can manage."

"No comment," Charlotte said. "I'll get the salad."

Peter stepped to the counter and picked up the breadbasket. "And I'll get the bread."

Ashley shrugged and smiled up at him. "There's nothing left for me to carry, so I guess I'll just tag along after you."

"Sure." For an instant, Peter thought Ashley was going to slip her arm in his just as she'd done a few minutes earlier with her father. He shut the thought down before it could go anywhere. What was his fascination with her today, anyway?

The question lingered in his mind as Richard indicated Peter should sit next to Ashley, while he and Charlotte sat on the opposite side of the table.

"Peter, you can say the blessing for the food," Richard said.

"Okay." Bowing his head, Peter wished his boss had asked his missionary daughter to say the prayer. Wasn't she better equipped for such duty? Was it right to ask God to help you say a prayer? Because that's what he planned to do before he opened his mouth. He didn't like praying aloud. He didn't do much praying, period, and that wasn't good. He hoped God would hear him now. *Lord, help me.*

Peter closed his eyes. "Thank you, Lord, for the blessings you've given each of us. We especially thank you for bringing Ashley home safely. Please be with those she left behind and help their country find peace. Thank you now for this food. In Jesus's name. Amen." After opening his eyes, he glanced at Ashley.

"Thank you for the prayer. I appreciate your mentioning the dear friends I had to leave. I wish I could've brought them all home with me." She smiled at him, and her eyes welled with tears again.

Peter had that strange urge once more to pull her into an embrace and comfort her. He gripped the arms of the chair to keep himself from acting on the thought. "It must've been hard."

She nodded. "The uprising was horrendous. So many people killed."

"Oh, my." Charlotte placed a hand over her heart as she passed the salad bowl. "You could've been injured or killed."

"We were warned to leave before the rebels reached us. They were targeting foreigners and killing innocent people at random."

"How did you escape?" Peter helped himself to a piece of bread and passed it on to Ashley.

Taking the breadbasket, she blinked back tears. "When we received the warning, we packed what we could. One of the local church members had an old truck. He packed three missionary families and me into the back and drove us to the border in the middle of the night. Once we crossed the border, we were safe. But I have no idea whether he had the opportunity to send our things. Or even if he's safe."

"I'm glad I didn't know any of this until now." Concern knitting his eyebrows, Richard served Charlotte some lasagna, then helped himself. "I had no idea you were in such danger."

"I'm not sure we knew at the time, either. We learned later how bad it was from the news reports we heard while we were waiting for our flights."

Sorry that he'd teased her about her clothes, Peter marveled at Ashley's bravery. Here was a young woman who didn't care about fashion or money. She cared about people, and she deserved his respect. She put him to shame. He picked up the serving fork for the lasagna. "May I serve you?"

Nodding, she held out her plate. "This looks so good. I may be tempted to eat too much. Maybe if I eat enough, I'll fit into these clothes."

"I was wondering about those. I thought Peter took you shopping." Richard helped himself to a bite of lasagna and looked intently at Ashley.

She gave her father a sheepish grin, then sighed. "He did, but I didn't want to mess with trying the stuff on. When I tried them on after my shower, I found out they were too big. I had to have something to wear tonight, but I can exchange the other things tomorrow. And I'll try them on this time."

Richard let out a big belly laugh. "The same old Ashley. Always in a hurry and not concerned about her clothes."

Throughout the rest of the meal, the conversation never returned to Ashley's departure from the mission field, but Peter couldn't get the tale of her escape out of his mind. Her courage was one more thing that intrigued him. Still, he had to remember she was the boss's daughter. She was too good for the likes of him. He needed to stay away from Ashley Hiatt.

Despite having to acknowledge her shopping blunder, Ashley appreciated not having to talk about her harrowing experiences. Enjoying her father's laughter, she didn't even mind that he and Peter were discussing the consequences of the runaway truck and their plans to deal with the damage. Maybe being back home would be okay. Or would this initial delight be short-lived?

"It's a great evening. Let's have dessert out on the patio or in the solarium." Richard got up from the table and proceeded toward the kitchen. "While we have cake, I have an important announcement."

"The solarium." Charlotte popped up from her chair. "That yellow pine pollen is covering everything on the patio."

Richard smiled and waited for Charlotte to go into the kitchen as he put a hand on her back. "You're right."

Ashley followed, wondering what kind of announcement her father was about to make. Did it have anything to do with the extremely friendly nature of his exchanges with Charlotte during the meal preparation and just now? Ashley wasn't sure what to make of it. While she was growing up, Ashley had never known her father to show a romantic interest in any woman. And as much as she loved Charlotte, a match between her father and their longtime housekeeper seemed odd. Ashley couldn't picture them together.

Entering the kitchen, Ashley looked over her shoulder. Peter lagged behind, anxiety clouding his expression. What was he thinking? Surely he wouldn't be concerned about her father's announcement, unless it had to do with business. She doubted it was business, because he wouldn't make that kind of announcement at home. He'd make it at work. Right?

Richard eyed Ashley. "Where's that little tiny piece of cake you were going to cut for me?"

"I'll have it ready in a minute." Ashley hurried to the counter where the cake was sitting and cut a very small piece, put it on a plate and handed it to her father.

Smiling wryly, he examined it. "Do you think you could've cut it any smaller?"

"Maybe. Would you like me to try?"

The big booming laugh she loved to hear filled the room. "No, because I believe you'd try. It's barely a mouthful as it is."

Ashley cut three more pieces and placed them on plates. "You said you didn't want to blow your diet. I only want to help."

"I know I have to be sensible. Doc wants me to keep the weight down." Richard led the group out to the solarium.

More new furniture filled the room, where early-evening sunshine spilled in through a wall of windows. Ashley placed the plate with her cake on the glass-topped wicker coffee table, then sat on the wicker sofa with floral-print upholstery. She wondered whether this diet talk meant her father had some kind of medical condition he wasn't telling her about. Maybe that was the big announcement.

Peter joined her on the sofa, while her father and Charlotte sat on the matching chairs on either side. Peter's prayer at dinner had touched her heart, but she still had reservations about the man.

For a few minutes, no one talked while they ate. Finally, Richard broke the silence. "Peter, I want you to help Ashley with her driving."

Wanting to slink away and hide, Ashley didn't dare look in Peter's direction. "Daddy, I don't need help with driving. I have a valid Georgia driver's license."

"You haven't driven in nearly five years. I can't let you out on the streets without some practice."

"I'm not sixteen. I don't need a chaperone." What must Peter think? Her father was foisting her on him at every turn. The man would hate the sight of her before the day was over. First, picking her up at the airport, then shopping, now driving lessons. Could it get any worse?

Richard eyed Peter. "You don't mind, do you?"

"No, sir. It would be my pleasure."

Ashley wanted to roll her eyes, but she resisted. Did Peter have any other response? He sounded as though he had one of those little pull strings in the back of his neck: Whenever her father asked Peter a question, someone pulled the string and the same answer came out of his mouth. Finally, she looked at him. "You really don't have to."

"I don't mind, honestly. You're dad's just thinking of your safety. A little driving practice can't hurt."

Charlotte shook her finger in Ashley's direction. "He's right, you know. The Atlanta traffic is bad enough for someone who drives in it all of the time. How will you do after being away so long?"

Ashley shrugged. They were all ganging up on her. Why fight it? Her father was determined that she have driving lessons, so driving lessons she would have. "Okay, I won't argue." *But that doesn't make me like it.* Forcing a smile, she bit back the words.

"I even bought you a new vehicle. It's being delivered to-morrow." Richard's statement shook Ashley from her thoughts.

"Thanks, Daddy. That was very thoughtful." Ashley again forced a smile, even though she wanted to scream. Once again, he was trying to run her life. If she complained, she'd sound like a spoiled brat. Her life had been so much simpler on the mission field. She would go back tomorrow if she could.

"If you're not satisfied, we'll get you something different," Richard said.

"I'm sure it'll be fine." Her father had always been the one in control. He liked to be in charge, but couldn't he remember she wasn't one of his employees that he could boss around like poor Peter? "Was that your big announcement?"

Richard burst out with his boisterous laugh again. "No. I just wanted to get that out of the way before I made the announcement."

"Why are you keeping me in suspense?" she asked, realizing how much she'd missed his laughter.

Richard glanced around the room until his gaze rested on Ashley again. "A little over a year ago, a good friend of mine suddenly died from a heart attack."

Ashley expelled a harsh breath. "You're not sick, are you?"

"No, no. I'm fine." He leaned over and patted Ashley's shoulder. "But it got me to thinking hard about my own life. You'd think with your dear mama passing away so young I would've been more aware of my mortality. Instead, I pushed it to the back of my mind." Blinking rapidly, Richard paused and rubbed his forehead. "I still miss her. Sometimes, I can still feel her presence in this house."

"Is that why you got rid of the old furniture? Because it reminded you of Mama?"

Richard shook his head. "I don't need furnishings to remind me of my sweet Katie. But the redecorating symbolized a new beginning for me. I decided I should turn my life in a new direction—make a new start."

"What does that mean?" Where was this headed, and why was he saying this stuff in front of Peter and Charlotte? Were they feeling a bit uncomfortable while her father talked about his personal midlife crisis? "Are you on a health kick now? Is that your new start?"

"That's part of it, but not all. After my friend died, I made an assessment of my life and decided that I haven't been a very good steward of the things God has blessed me with. I accumulated a lot of wealth, and it is about time I used it for God."

"How do you plan to do that?" Ashley asked, casting a surreptitious glance in Peter's direction. His expression was blank. What did he think of her father's pronouncement? She'd always seen Peter as a person who was looking to get ahead however he could. Even now he was her father's yes-man.

"I talked with our pastor about using my money to do something besides sending it to missions. After a lot of prayer and consultation with area pastors, I saw a need I could fill."

"What's that?"

"I've set up a mission to fund some very special projects, and I want you to be part of the operation. Peter, too."

Ashley stared at her father. "You want me to *what?*"

"I know you're unhappy about having to leave your mission teaching, but look at this as another opportunity to serve God."

"Daddy, did you ever think I might not want to do this? You can't plan everyone's life without consulting with them first." Ashley looked at Peter. His expression mirrored her own dismay.

"Sir, what exactly do you mean? Am I out at Hiatt Construction?"

Steepling his hands in front of him, Richard leaned back in his chair and glanced from one to the other. "Okay, I can see this has caught you both off guard."

Ashley leaned forward. "Yes, you could say that. I just got home, and you're telling me I have to be part of your special project, without consulting me *or* Peter." She glanced in Peter's direction. He didn't look happy, either. "Are you going to explain?"

Richard rubbed his hands together, then clasped them. "I'm so excited about this that I forgot you don't know any details."

Ashley frowned. "Then give us the details."

"I will. Be patient." He patted her hand. "My mind is whirling with the possibilities, and your coming home at just this time makes it all the better." Richard stood and started pacing the floor. "I need someone to oversee the project, and you need somewhere to serve." Eyeing Ashley, he stopped pacing and waved emphatically with his hands. "Your being here is an answer to my prayers. You and Peter will make a great team."

"How do I fit into this project?" Peter's eyebrows knit with a little frown.

Peter and her—a team? Was that possible? Thankfully, those words didn't come blurting out of her mouth while she waited for her father's explanation.

"Here's the plan." Richard started pacing again. "We're going to use the foundation to fund projects to help repair, paint and rebuild houses for elderly folks and poor families." He stopped and looked at her again. "There are a number of projects in the inner city, but I want to do something in small towns. People forget folks are suffering in rural areas as well as the big cities."

"What small towns?" Ashley asked as she tried to absorb her father's explanation.

"Towns in the north Georgia mountains." Richard pointed northward. "I've already spoken to several church leaders in the area, and they've identified people who need help."

Ashley scooted forward on the sofa. "So what are we doing? Going up there with our hammers and paintbrushes? I don't think anyone wants me to help them build or paint anything."

Richard chuckled. "It'll be a good learning experience."

"Are you serious? How can two people, one totally inexperienced with construction, complete any of these projects?"

Her father walked over and patted her head. "It's not just you two, sugar. We're going to have youth groups, church groups, families and individuals who are looking for a short-term mission project do the work. You'll be working with the church leaders up there. They'll help you schedule groups and make arrangements for housing, meals and transportation. Church families will take those volunteers who need housing into their homes. I have a prospectus with details about everything."

"And how do I get the groups?"

"We've already developed literature and distributed it to churches in a mass mailing, and we've set up a Web site. We already have a number of groups lined up, starting in the middle of May and continuing through the summer."

"I'm in charge of that, too?"

"Yes." Her father motioned toward Peter. "And I want to put Peter in charge of the financial management of the project— getting the supplies, paying the bills, et cetera."

"This sounds like a wonderful opportunity for both of you." Charlotte got up and stacked the empty plates and forks. "I'll take these to the kitchen."

Ashley wished she could escape with Charlotte instead of having her father plan her life. Was this God's plan or just her father's? "I'm not sure I'm ready to do what you're asking. All I know is teaching."

"That experience will help you." Richard looked at Peter. "Peter has great business sense, and I have confidence the two of you will do well together."

"I'll have to pray about this," Ashley said, dreading the idea of having to deal with Peter day in and day out. Despite her strange reactions to him today, weren't they like oil and water? They didn't mix, but her father was determined to throw them together.

Richard wagged an index finger at her. "That's exactly what you should do. All of us should make it a matter of prayer."

Did that mean Peter, too? She glanced his way. Weariness overcame her as she tried to balance all of her conflicting feelings. She was too tired to make any important decisions tonight. Maybe this would look more feasible after a good night's sleep and a whole lot of prayer.

Chapter Four

The early morning sun beamed through the sidelights in the foyer, where Peter waited for Ashley. Two days after Richard requested that Peter help Ashley with her driving, they had plans to take their first test drive. Expecting her to appear at any moment, he drummed the fingers of one hand on the banister and gazed up the stairway.

He never imagined she'd be late. He'd always seen her as punctual. Was she wishing he wasn't here? Her objection to her father's request made Peter wonder how long he'd be waiting. Nothing about the situation pleased him, but he had to make the best of it. Somehow he needed to make Ashley feel as though this wasn't a test of her driving skills.

When Peter arrived, Richard had answered the door, then made his excuses as he headed out for his regular Saturday morning round of golf. Peter was left to deal with Ashley alone. As he waited for his reluctant pupil to show her face, the quiet house echoed with the tick, tick, tick of the grandfather clock in the foyer. Was she so reluctant that she'd gone down the back stairs and out of the house?

Enough foolish thinking. He'd done a lot of that over the

past couple of days. For the first time since he'd come to work for Hiatt Construction, he had no idea where he stood with his boss. Shaking his head, Peter stepped into the living room and looked out the front window. Sunbeams radiated through the tall pines and gave a dream-world effect to the expansive front yard. Were his plans for advancement at the company a dream as well?

Richard had never given Peter an answer to the question about his status with the company. He didn't have a good feeling about anything—his job, today's outing or his future. For over fifteen years, he'd devoted his life to Hiatt Construction. He'd always pictured himself stepping into Richard Hiatt's shoes one day as head of the company. Now that seemed unlikely.

Richard was shuffling him off to manage a mission project, while Mark Becker took over Peter's responsibilities at the construction company. His hopes and dreams for the future had just evaporated. With these doubts swirling through his mind, Peter was tempted to do something he'd never done before— say no to his boss. Since the mission scenario seemed to point to an abrupt halt to his potential rise within the company, what was the point in saying yes to this?

Hurried footsteps sounded on the stairs. As Peter turned, Ashley took the last two steps in one bound, her sneaker-clad feet landing with a thud on the hardwood floor.

Glancing around, she spotted him and grinned sheepishly. "I'm sorry to keep you waiting. I'm not usually late."

"I didn't wait that long."

"Good. I was reading and lost track of the time."

"I thought maybe you'd skipped out on me."

Eyes wide, she looked up at him. "Why would you think that?"

Peter laughed. "You have to ask?"

"No, I guess not."

"I see you've been shopping again."

"Yes." Arms stretched wide, she twirled in a circle. "Everything fits. Do you approve?"

He didn't miss the hint of sarcasm in her question. Should he tell her she looked great in the faded blue jeans and red knit top, or was that going too far? He wasn't sure what to say or how to act around the boss's daughter. Almost everything about this morning was unexpected, especially Ashley's actions and appearance. "Yeah."

"Thanks." She let out a loud sigh. "We might as well get started." She trotted off toward the kitchen without waiting for him. "The dealer delivered the pickup last night."

Did she say "pickup"? He hurried after her. "You didn't give it a trial run last night?"

"No, I believe my dad's a little frightened to get in a vehicle of any kind with me at the wheel."

Peter narrowed his gaze. "Why?"

She gave him another sheepish grin. "I think he remembers the times he rode shotgun when I had my learner's permit. I think he described it as a 'white-knuckle nightmare.'"

Peter couldn't help chuckling. "It was that bad?"

Ashley nodded. "Especially after I had a little mishap with the wall in the garage."

"Would you care to elaborate?"

"Maybe, if you quit grinning." She grabbed a set of keys off the hook near the door leading to the garage.

"Okay. My expression is blank." He stopped short on the threshold. A candy-apple red, extended-cab pickup truck gleamed in the sunlight streaming in through the row of windows in the garage door. "You did say 'pickup,' didn't you? I thought maybe I'd misunderstood you."

"It's a pickup all right."

"Why did your dad buy you a pickup?"

"What did you expect—a fancy sports car?"

"Frankly, yes."

Ashley chuckled. "Daddy told me a pickup would be much more useful for hauling supplies for the mission project."

"Makes sense. Are you okay with driving it?"

"I don't know." Shrugging, she smiled and punched the button that triggered the garage door opener. "Are you sure you want to take your chances with me behind the wheel? Daddy will never know if you don't."

"But I'll know. I couldn't look your dad in the eye if I didn't do what he asked."

"I know what you mean. I could never lie to him, either."

"You mean the missionary considered telling a lie?"

"I wasn't a missionary then, but just because I've been a missionary doesn't mean I'm not tempted to do the wrong thing. Please don't put me on a pedestal." Ashley hopped behind the wheel.

Peter got in and buckled his seat belt. "That wasn't my intention."

"Good. I have as many faults as the next person, so I don't want you thinking of me as something I'm not." She turned the key in the ignition. The engine roared to life.

"You can count on that." *Or could she?* He wasn't sure how to treat her or what to expect from her. She had his emotions tied in knots.

With her hair pulled into a ponytail, she looked tiny, young and vulnerable. She was shorter than Peter had remembered. He was tempted to tease her and suggest she get a booster seat, but that wouldn't win him any points.

His heart took a funny little leap when she gripped the steering wheel and looked at him with those big amber eyes. She was the boss's daughter. What was going on with him? She wasn't even his type.

"Are you ready?" she asked.

"The real question is, are *you* ready?"

"Absolutely. Where should we go?"

"How about a drive around the subdivision?"

She gave him a perturbed glance. "The subdivision? You're as bad as my dad."

Peter laughed. "Humor me, okay?"

"Sure. I'll try not to rip off the side mirror as I back out." She put the pickup in reverse and looked over her shoulder.

Was that a bit of irritation he heard in her voice? Maybe he wasn't dealing with this assignment so well. Holding his breath, Peter tried not to do the white-knuckle routine as she slowly backed the pickup out of the garage.

"Well, what do you know? I didn't hit anything."

Peter decided not to comment on her sarcasm. Could he blame her? She was an adult and didn't enjoy being treated like a kid. "That's a good start."

"Are you trying to imitate my dad, or have you just worked for him so long that you've begun to sound like him?" Ashley proceeded down the driveway.

"I sound like your dad?"

"You do." She stopped at the end of the drive and looked both ways.

"I consider that a compliment. Your dad's a great man. I'd be proud to have him for a father."

She turned onto the street. "He's a great father, but sometimes he can be very irritating."

Peter chuckled. "Are you saying in a roundabout way that I'm irritating?"

"Now you're putting words in my mouth."

"No, just trying to clarify. If we're going to work together, I ought to know where I stand."

Ashley didn't respond but continued to drive through the streets of the subdivision in silence until she had covered the neighborhood. Peter remained silent also, not wanting to distract her from the task at hand—driving the pickup that seemed way too big for her.

Finally, she returned home. She pulled to a stop in front of the garage and turned off the engine. Gripping the steering wheel, she looked straight ahead. "Did I pass, or are there more tests?"

Sunlight filtered through the shiny new leaves of spring as Peter stared at the trees lining the driveway. Why had he made her go through this silly exercise? She'd handled the pickup with ease, but would it be the same on a busy street?

He'd definitely gotten off to a bad start with Ashley today. She probably thought he was overbearing and insufferable. Why did he care? Because in the end, despite his doubts, he was going to honor his boss's request to do this mission project. If he intended to work with her, they needed to come to an understanding. But was there something more? He pushed the question away before it could settle.

"That wasn't a test. Just a chance for you to get a feel for driving a pickup," Peter said as he tried to decide on his next step.

Did he dare ask her to explain the incident with the garage wall? After all, she'd brought it up. And she'd never answered his question as to whether she considered him irritating. Did her lack of response mean she'd decided to defy her father and not do the mission project? Peter immediately dismissed that scenario. She wouldn't be talking about using the pickup for supplies if that was the case.

The determined set of her jaw as she continued to stare straight ahead didn't bode well for her acceptance of his plans for the day. Would she balk because they were his ideas and not hers? The questions were piling up in his mind like discarded lumber at a construction site.

Normally he considered himself an assured man who didn't have a problem with telling people what he thought. He had nearly an entire company under his command, or at least he had until a couple of days ago. Maybe that was the problem. His ego was suffering a crisis of confidence.

He had to quit letting one young woman intimidate him. He forced himself to remain nonchalant. "You never told me what happened with the garage wall."

Turning his way, she gave him an impish grin. "Were you thinking about that the whole time I was driving?"

"Only when you were backing out of the garage."

She laid her head back on the headrest and laughed out loud. "I forgot to look for the white knuckles."

"None here." He wiggled his fingers, then waved a hand in front of his face. "And you can see I'm not grinning or smiling."

"Okay, when I had my learner's permit, I drove into the garage like I'd done hundreds of times before while I was practicing to get my license. As I stepped on the brake, my foot slipped and landed back on the accelerator. Suddenly, we were zooming into the wall. Daddy bellowed at the top of his lungs, and I managed to stop before I sent the car crashing through the wall."

Not daring to look at Ashley, Peter forced himself not to laugh. When he finally gained control, he glanced her way. "How much damage?"

"Just a big hole in the drywall. Daddy had one of his guys come out and patch the hole and paint."

"Was he angry?"

"No, he got a big kick out of telling his friends *and* my friends. I was mortified."

Peter chuckled, then grimaced. "Didn't mean to laugh."

Ashley shook her head. "That's okay. Daddy and I both laugh about it now, but at the time I wanted to hide."

"Was this little story a warning that I should get out before you drive into the garage?"

Narrowing her gaze, she stared at him. "So I'm done?"

"I didn't say that."

"Then what do you mean?"

"Do I take it from your comments that you plan to work with your father's mission project?"

Ashley nodded. "God closed a door in Africa, but he has opened a door here. I really had to pray about it, and I also needed a little time to let the idea soak in. I really loved the work and people I was with over the past five years."

Peter was beginning to comprehend her pain. He had some of the same feelings about leaving his position with Hiatt Construction. He couldn't tell her and didn't dare admit he hadn't taken time to pray. His decision was all about pleasing Richard, not necessarily pleasing God. She'd prayed about her decision. He'd stewed over his. Would there ever come a time when he'd rely on God as she did?

Hoping to steer his mind away from those troubling thoughts, he said, "Have you read the mission project prospectus?"

"The prospectus?"

"Yeah. Your dad's plan." The way she asked the question told Peter she probably hadn't looked beyond the cover. How would she react to *his* plan for the day?

"I haven't looked at it." Ashley wished she could start the day over. First, she'd been late. Then she'd had to prove her driving skills to Peter, her father's handsome yes-man. Now she had to admit she hadn't read the prospectus. She wanted to rely on prayer and God's leading, but business types like her father and Peter operated with spreadsheets, reports and bottom lines.

"No problem." Peter shrugged his shoulders. "It was mainly a lot of numbers and projections."

"Are you sure?" Did he think she was a slacker because she hadn't bothered with the prospectus?

"Yes, but I'd like to do some research myself."

"What does that involve?"

"A trip to north Georgia."

"When?"

"How about today? Are you ready to drive?"

Trying to hide a smile, she stared at him. "You want me to drive?"

"Sure."

"You're a very trusting man."

"Are you telling me you're not ready to drive?"

"Oh, I'm ready. I'm just surprised you're ready to let me." He laughed. "You appear perfectly capable of driving to me."

"Thanks." She grinned. Unlike her father, Peter was giving her a vote of confidence.

"Would you like to know what we're doing when we get there?"

"Yes." She suddenly realized, despite his assessment that she was a capable driver, Peter was more like her father than she wanted to admit. Peter wanted to run things, too. He wanted to tell her where to go and what to do when she got there. Did that mean she had to go along with his plan? Everything in her wanted to resist whatever agenda he had in mind, but she was sure God didn't want her to take that attitude. This was about serving Him, not her own wishes.

"The list of contacts for the projects was in the prospectus. So I called and talked with several of them. I arranged to meet with a couple of them this afternoon."

"And you were going to do this with or without me?"

For a moment, Peter looked startled, as he appeared to contemplate her question. "I didn't think of it that way. I'm just used to being in charge, so I made plans."

As Ashley listened to Peter's explanation, she knew the word *sorry* wasn't going to cross his lips. Men like him did what they wanted and made excuses later. "Well, from now on, if we're going to work together, I'd like to be included in the plans before they're made for me. Is that okay with you?"

"Absolutely. I'll make a note of it. Let's head out."

"Let me grab a jacket and write a note to Daddy before we go."

"You could give him a call on his cell."

"I'll leave him a note. As I recall, he doesn't like to be disturbed on the golf course."

Peter nodded. "I'll wait right here."

He'd make a note of it. With that response to her request, she'd have to make a note to remind him when he got overbearing. As she hurried into the house, Ashley stopped short. Here she was again having an unfair reaction toward Peter's viewpoint. With a heavy sigh, she said a short prayer. *Lord, help me to keep my cool when Peter starts ordering me around.*

Arguing with the man probably wasn't a good idea, but she wasn't going to let him walk all over her, either. She had to stand up for herself, or she was sure he'd bowl right over her with his take-charge attitude. Still, she had to do it with a gentle spirit. She needed God's help to accomplish that task.

When Ashley returned, Peter was studying a map. "Where'd you get the map?"

"From my car." Peter glanced up at her. "I wanted to make sure we know where we're going."

"I hope the traffic isn't too bad."

"Once we get away from the city it'll probably be okay."

"Let's hope so." Ashley tossed her jacket in the backseat.

"Do you want me to give you directions to 400?"

"No."

"You remember how to get there?"

Ashley drove onto the street. "I don't have to. Look in my backpack. Daddy bought me a GPS unit, as well as a cell phone. He's trying to bring me into the world of fancy gadgets. You can program our destination into the GPS."

"We're definitely going to have to retrain you on the communication front." Peter chuckled as he opened the backpack and pulled out a little leather case. "Is this it?"

"Yes," Ashley answered, trying not to let his retraining comment bother her.

Peter shuffled through the portfolio on his lap. Finally, he pulled out a piece of paper. "Got the address right here. Would you like to stop in Helen for lunch?"

"Sure. I haven't been to Helen since I was a little girl." She gave him a sideways glance.

"Good. I'll program it into the GPS. Then we can go from Helen to our final destination."

"Great." Ashley stopped as she reached the entrance to the subdivision. Was she really ready to drive? The pickup had been easy to handle on the quiet streets of her neighborhood, but what about the busy roads leading out of the city? For all of her earlier bravado, suddenly she wasn't so sure about her driving ability. She gave herself a mental shake. She shouldn't let her father's assessment undermine her confidence.

Glancing in the rearview mirror to make sure she wasn't blocking traffic, Ashley waited for Peter to program the GPS and get it mounted on the dash. When he finished, he turned to her. "We're set. Looks like it'll take us about an hour and a half to get there, as long as we don't run into any bad traffic."

"It's Saturday, so we shouldn't have to deal with people driving to work." Ashley listened to the instructions from the automated female voice as it told her to turn left onto Roswell Road. Looking left and right, she said a silent prayer for safety before making the turn.

In minutes they were headed north on Georgia 400. While Ashley drove, Peter studied papers he'd pulled from his portfolio. Did she dare ask what he was doing? Did it have something to do with the mission project, or was it Hiatt Construction business?

Just drive and forget Peter is even here. She didn't want to notice him, but everything about him seemed larger than life as he sat beside her in the truck.

If they were going to work together, she had to get used to having him around. That meant putting him in the proper perspective. They didn't have much in common, and he certainly wasn't going to look at her as a potential romantic interest, not that she had any interest in such a development. So letting her thoughts dwell on him was ridiculous.

All of the women she'd ever seen him date were tall, with long, sleek hair, shapely figures and beautiful faces. With frizzy hair, glasses and a freckled nose, Ashley didn't have any dreams of competing with those women for his attention. But she couldn't deny he was hard to ignore, with his handsome face and devastating smile.

"Hey, you're doing a great job with the driving." His voice startled her from her thoughts.

"Thanks. Be sure to tell Daddy. That'll put his mind at ease." Laughing, she hoped Peter couldn't read her mind.

As she drove away from the city, she relaxed and glanced occasionally at the scenery. In the distance the Blue Ridge Mountains rose above the Georgia Piedmont like the great humps of some prehistoric animal. As they neared Helen, the deep blue-green of the pines accented the much lighter green of the barely visible new leaves in the hardwood forest surrounding them.

Ashley breathed a sigh of relief when they arrived in Helen. While Peter put away his papers, she found a parking place near the main street that sported shops and restaurants built to resemble an alpine village. "Do you know a good place to eat?"

"I've never been here, but I say let's go to one of the places serving German food."

"Bratwurst. One of my favorite."

"I agree." Ashley picked up the GPS. "I'll put this in my backpack until we're ready to go again."

"Good idea." She handed it to him.

When he took it from her, their fingers brushed. Just like on the day he'd picked her up from the airport, the contact made her heart race. All of the instruction she'd given herself about not noticing him or letting him affect her floated away in the fresh mountain air.

Scrambling out of the pickup, she gave herself another mental pep talk about her unexpected fascination with Peter Dalton. It couldn't lead to anything good. When he joined her on the sidewalk, she forced the crazy thoughts about him out of her mind. Business was the order of the day. *She* should make a note of *that*.

As they walked together toward the restaurant, she wondered whether this attraction should be a matter for prayer. And if it was, how should she pray? *Lord, I think I'm in trouble. Please help me with this situation.*

When they reached the restaurant, Peter smiled and held open the door for her. He was a gentleman, and that made it harder to be immune to him. She had to keep telling herself that being drawn to the charms of a handsome man meant nothing.

After they were seated and the waitress took their drink order, Ashley buried her nose in the menu so she wouldn't have to look at Peter. Maybe that would help. The menu listed a number of sausages: bauernwurst, bratwusrt, knackwurst, rindswurst and weisswurst, as well as schnitzel, kraut and Hungarian stew. None of the dishes sounded good at the moment, because her stomach was tied in knots.

"What looks good to you?" Peter asked.

"Maybe the schnitzel or Hungarian stew." She wondered whether she could actually eat either. "What about you?"

"Bratwurst. One of my favorites."

The waitress returned and took their order. She left, taking the menus with her. Now Ashley had nothing to hide behind. What should she do? Was this where she had to make small talk, actually get to know Peter? Maybe getting to know him would take away the attraction. Or would that only make it worse? The questions rippled through her mind like the Chattahoochee River flowing outside the window next to their table.

Maybe she should ask Peter about her father and Charlotte. Hopefully, that would steer her thoughts in a totally new direction. Would he know whether something was going on between them? The fact that she didn't know made her realize she hadn't been in touch with her father's life, despite their frequent e-mails and weekly phone calls.

She hadn't known what he'd done to the house, and she surely didn't know what was happening or not happening in his love life. What kind of daughter had to ask one of his employees what was going on in her father's life?

Even though she had been on another continent with an ocean between them, she should've pressed her dad for more details. She'd let him get away with perfunctory facts about what he was doing. Mostly he talked about work, and she'd let it go at that, because she thought that was his only interest.

Peter was her father's close work associate. Surely he would know what was happening. She had to ask. Before she could get the question out of her mouth, however, the waitress brought their order.

Immediately, Peter started eating. After he'd taken a couple of bites, he looked up at her. "You aren't eating. Aren't you…oh, yeah, I forgot. You probably pray before meals, even in restaurants. Would you like to pray now?"

"Sure." Bowing her head and closing her eyes, Ashley said a short prayer of thanksgiving for the food.

"You'll have to keep me in line while we work together." Peter still wore an embarrassed expression as he resumed eating.

Ashley doubted there was going to be any chance of that. He'd do what he wanted. "I think you can keep yourself in line. Besides, you're doing it again."

"Doing what again?"

"Making me into this person who always does the right thing. I don't always remember to pray when I eat out."

"So I'm not on your bad list then?"

Shaking her head, Ashley laughed halfheartedly. "I don't have a bad list."

"That's good to know. I want us to get along, since we'll be spending a lot of time together."

Spending a lot of time together. Was she ready for that? Frowning, Ashley cut a piece of her schnitzel and stabbed it with a fork. "You're making me sound like someone who's hard to deal with."

Peter grimaced and raked a hand through his short sandy-brown hair. "I didn't mean that. Can we forget this conversation and start a new topic?"

"That suits me. Is there anything going on between my dad and Charlotte?"

Chapter Five

Trying not to choke on his brat, Peter swallowed very slowly. That was a change of topic—one he'd never anticipated. Funny how he'd wondered the same thing. Why did she expect him to know, when she didn't? Since both Ashley and he were wondering, maybe a romance *had* developed between his boss and the housekeeper.

Peter ran a hand through his hair again. If he kept this up, he'd be bald soon. So far today his dealings with Ashley had brought him nothing but inner turmoil. Did he dare voice his suspicions? He didn't have anything to go on except the exchange he'd witnessed the other night at dinner.

"What makes you ask?"

She didn't say anything for a moment. She just stared at him, her eyes wide behind her glasses. Then she let her gaze drop as she took another bite of her food.

Finally, she looked back at him. "Well, I noticed a…I don't know how to explain it. I just know their interaction at dinner the other night was different from the way they acted toward each other before I went away." Pausing, Ashley waved a hand in the air. "There was this chummy undercurrent to their inter-action. Am I way off base?"

"Maybe not."

Ashley raised her eyebrows. "So you're saying there is something going on between them?"

Shrugging, Peter shook his head. "I don't know for sure, but I noticed that they talk to each other more like friends than boss and employee."

"So what should I do?"

"You're asking me?" Peter pointed to himself. "He's your father."

Ashley sighed. "I don't know whether I should mention it. I'd feel silly if there's nothing going on."

"Then your only choice is to wait and see what happens."

"I guess I'll have to. Safer that way." Ashley started eating again.

They ate in silence. While Peter finished his meal, he glanced at Ashley. She ate like a starving woman, not making eye contact at all. Was she embarrassed to have asked about her father and Charlotte?

He thought for a moment about the trauma of her homecom-ing. First, she'd had the shock of the cruel circumstances that required her to leave the mission field in such a hurry. Then she had to deal with being thrust into this new mission that involved working with someone she barely knew. And she was worried about what was happening with her father. All of this would make anyone feel off balance. But for the most part, she seemed to be handling it pretty well. He had to admire her spunk.

"You'll tell me if you learn something, won't you?" Ashley's question startled Peter from his thoughts.

"You mean about your father?"

"Yeah."

"You're his daughter. Don't you think he'd mention something like that to you first?"

"Maybe. I just thought there might be some man-to-man talk between you."

"We rarely talk about personal stuff. Just business."

"Oh." Tilting her head, she looked thoughtful. "Since we're going to be working together, would it bother you if I asked you personal questions?"

Peter laughed halfheartedly. "That depends on how personal the questions get."

"Not that personal." She made a nervous gesture with her hands as a pink tinge crept across her cheeks and freckled nose. "I just thought since we'd be working together that I should get to know you better."

"Okay. What do you want to know?"

Ashley bit her bottom lip and stared at him, the pink still staining her cheeks.

"Well?"

She shrugged. "I…I don't know. When I think of something, I'll ask, okay?"

"Sure." Now he'd gone and embarrassed her. He didn't want her to feel awkward around him, but he wasn't sure how to deal with the situation himself. A fine team they were going to make.

Before they could continue their conversation, the waitress brought the check. They both reached for it. Peter snatched it first. "Your dad gave me a credit card especially for the mission work. This meal should go on that."

"Fine," she said, but her smile was forced.

While he paid the bill, Peter wondered why it bothered Ashley that her father was paying for the meal. Maybe she was upset that her father had given him the credit card rather than her. Possibly he was reading something into her reaction that wasn't there at all.

But knowing the history between Ashley and her father made Peter believe she wasn't happy about being under her father's care. He'd seen her independent streak from the beginning. He only had to look at her shopping trip for evidence.

After Peter paid the bill, he stood. "Let's get going. I told them we'd be there by two o'clock."

Ashley fished the keys out of her backpack and handed them to him.

"You want me to drive?"

"No. I gave you the keys so you have access to the pickup if you want to wait there." She started to leave, then turned back. "I'm going to the restroom. Then I want to shop a little before we go. I won't be long."

Peter stared after her. *She wants to shop?* Something wasn't right. Was this the same woman who didn't want to shop for clothes? Now she wanted to spend time looking through souvenir shops? He didn't know what to make of Ashley Hiatt. Just when he thought he had her figured out, she did something completely out of character. Was she constantly going to keep him guessing?

Ashley hurried along the sidewalk and stopped short when she saw Peter sporting a pair of sunglasses. He lounged against the pickup, his arms crossed. He seemed bored as he looked up the street. Her heart did one of those little flip-flops that had become part of being around him. She hated to think a handsome face was turning her head. She knew character was more important than looks, but the message wasn't getting to her heart.

Just as she started to say something, he looked her way. "Ready?"

She hoped he didn't notice she'd been staring at him. She glanced at her watch. "How much time do I have?"

"No speed shopping today?" He grinned.

Would the shopping episode that had resulted in her ill-fitting clothes be a source of amusement for weeks to come? "I can be as speedy as I need to be."

"Good." He pulled his cell phone out of his pocket and looked at it. "We need to leave in thirty minutes."

"That'll require speed shopping."

"I didn't expect you'd want to shop."

"You don't have any sisters, do you?"

He gave her a puzzled frown. "No, I have two brothers."

"Just as I thought."

"Why do you say that?"

"Even though I'm not like a lot of women you know, please don't treat me like one of the guys."

He looked completely clueless. "Was I treating you like a guy?"

Ashley stifled a laugh. "Not exactly, but you were going to rush off without giving me a chance to check out the shops."

"But you don't like to shop."

"Not for myself, but I like to shop for other people. I wanted to pick up a few little gifts for the women I served with on the mission."

"Be my guest." Peter gestured for her to go ahead. "You can't fault me for judging you based on my experience from the other day."

"I suppose not."

"I'll meet you back here in thirty minutes."

"Okay." Ashley hurried off, disappointed that Peter wasn't going with her. *Stupid, stupid, stupid.* Why would he care about shopping with her? This day was turning out to be more of a challenge than she'd anticipated. She wished it were over. If she couldn't handle one day dealing with Peter, how was she going to survive working with him for the unforeseeable future?

When she entered a shop featuring blown glass, a clear glass cross trimmed in gold caught her eye. She went to examine it more closely and discovered a verse on a plaque next to the cross. The verse, Proverbs 3:5, read: "Trust in the Lord with all your heart and lean not on your own understanding."

She stepped back for a moment and whispered the verse. The message was clear. Worries about dealing with Peter crowded her mind because she hadn't been trusting in the Lord. Why was it so easy to forget to lean on God? He was right there all the time waiting to help, and she'd been trying to take care of everything on her own. The cross and verse would remind her to trust in God.

After she found three more items, she quickly made her purchases and headed back. Peter was still there, leaning against the pickup as if he'd never left. But he had a little bag in one hand and his cell phone in the other.

When she drew nearer, he glanced at the cell phone. "You're right on time."

"Did you expect me to be late?"

"My shopping experience with women has taught me that they are seldom on time." Before she could protest, he held up one hand. "But I know, other than this morning, I should always expect you to be on time. And you aren't like other women, with one exception. You like to shop, as long as it's fast."

Chuckling, Ashley opened the driver's side door. "Okay, so I was late this morning, and you've got me pegged."

Peter joined her in the cab of the pickup. "I didn't mean anything by that. I was trying to remind myself not to treat you like one of the guys."

Ashley couldn't help laughing. "I deserved that."

"I don't know what you deserve, but I bought you a gift."

Ashley's heart skipped a beat as she took the bag from him. Why was he buying her gifts? "What's the occasion?"

He shrugged. "I saw it and thought of you."

Holding her breath, she opened the bag and peered inside. She lifted out a key ring attached to a string of colorful beads with a crystal cross at the end. She held it up, then glanced at Peter. "Thank you. It's lovely."

"I wandered into the little shop right here and saw the key chain. I thought you needed something nicer than this plastic thing the car dealer gave your dad." He held up her keys. "Would you like me to put your keys on the new ring?"

"Yes, thank you." She wanted to tell him he shouldn't be buying her gifts, but that would be ungrateful. What had prompted him to do it? What other surprising things would she learn about Peter in the days to come?

Sunlight glinted off the pickup's hood as they drove up the hilly street in the small north Georgia town. Peter read the house numbers as the voice on the GPS indicated their arrival at their destination. "We're here."

Ashley stopped the pickup behind a gray sedan and a white SUV parked in front of a two-story white clapboard house with a big front porch. She glanced at Peter. "Who lives here?"

"Actually, I'm not sure. They only gave me the address where we're supposed to meet."

"Who are we meeting?"

He looked at the paper in his hand, then at the house. "A Pastor Cummings, a Mr. Floyd and a Mrs. Weaver. We're here a few minutes early."

"Good. Since you've read the prospectus and made all the plans, I'll let you do the talking."

Peter suddenly felt unprepared—a feeling he'd seldom had since coming to work for Hiatt Construction. But he was definitely out of his element here. He'd jumped into this thing without his usual detailed preparation, and he hadn't included

Ashley in his decisions. Now he realized his mistake. What was he doing here? He didn't know anything. Despite his limited knowledge, he was determined to make this meeting productive. "Okay, if that's the way you want it."

"I do."

Was her request a subtle way of reminding him that he hadn't included her in the plans? Guilt produced the unkind thought. He shook it away. Even though he didn't know her that well, he knew she didn't operate that way.

As they approached the door, Peter told himself that Ashley didn't fault him for not including her in the preparations. Even when she'd asked him to inform her of future plans, she did it with kindness.

How did she maintain her gentle spirit? That was a stupid question. She'd served for five years in the mission field. Her relationship with God was front and center. He, on the other hand, had lots of work to do in regard to *his* relationship with God.

God certainly had a sense of humor. Wait until he told his parents and his brothers that he was doing mission work instead of moving up the company ladder. They wouldn't believe it.

Peter rang the bell. A tall man with graying black hair answered the door. Peter stepped forward and extended his hand. "Hello, I'm Peter Dalton, and this is Ashley Hiatt."

The man smiled. "I'm Rob Cummings. It's so good to meet you. Come right in, everyone's here. Thanks for driving up today. We're eager to get started."

Rob led them into the living room, where a gray-haired man and a middle-aged woman with copper-red hair sat on a muted green sofa. He quickly made the introductions, and Peter took in the genuine enthusiasm of Charlie Floyd and Teresa Weaver. There were no false faces in this group. This was nothing like the business meetings he was used to, where people had to feel each other out and make calculated decisions about the motives and agendas behind the smiles and handshakes. He'd have to develop a whole new mindset.

The meeting started with prayer. Then they spent an hour going over the plans and explaining the facilities available for their use during the projects. Peter listened to Ashley's quiet but insightful comments with a growing appreciation that she was on his team. As she'd requested, she let him do most of the talking. Yet even though things seemed to be going well, he had the feeling something would pop up that he couldn't handle.

Finally, Rob suggested they look at one of the houses on the project list. Peter jumped at a reason to end the meeting that made him uncomfortable. He couldn't put his finger on the source of his unease, but it sat in his mind like a huge boulder that needed to be removed from a construction site. Maybe looking at the house they'd be renovating would put him more in his element.

Rob led the way as they walked out to the vehicles. "Y'all follow me. It's not far."

"We'll be right behind you." Ashley got into the pickup and turned to Peter. "You did a good job with the meeting. I'm glad one of us was prepared."

"Thanks. I appreciated your input, too." Peter didn't know whether to be complimented or chastised. He should quit trying to read anything into her statements. "How do you feel about staying with the Weavers and their two teenage girls?"

"I think it'll be great. I hope they won't consider it an inconvenience to have a constant houseguest."

"They wouldn't have volunteered to do it if they considered it an inconvenience."

"I hope you're right. I can hardly wait to meet the girls. I wish they'd been home today." Ashley pulled to a stop behind

Pastor Rob's sedan at the traffic light. "After my mom died, I always wished my dad would get married again so I could have some brothers and sisters. So for me, this will be like having a couple of sisters."

Peter heard the wistful tone in Ashley's voice. Had she been a lonely child? Charlotte had indicated that Ashley as a child had seemed more interested in books than in people. Maybe getting lost in books had been her way of coping with the loneliness after her mother's death.

"Having siblings isn't always fun. My brothers and I had our share of fights while we were growing up." How often had he taken his brothers for granted when they were kids, even into their adult years? He hadn't appreciated his brothers until he'd almost lost them to war injuries and cancer.

"I wouldn't even mind that part. It's an element of family life I missed. But I did experience some of the give and take between siblings while I was living with a missionary family that had young children."

"So you know a little about having brothers and sisters, do you?"

"A little." She chuckled. "Are you okay living at the pastor's house?"

"Sure, but I suppose I'll have to be on my best behavior." Peter grinned at Ashley as she parked the pickup behind Pastor Rob's car as he pulled to the curb. "Of course, I have to be on my best behavior no matter what because I'll be working with you."

Shutting off the engine, she narrowed her gaze. "You're doing it again."

He gave her a wink, then laughed. "I know, but I can't help teasing you."

"If that's the case, then you aren't trying very hard to be on your best behavior."

"You got me there." Peter opened the door and got out. How was he was going to manage living at the pastor's house? Life would definitely be different. He'd never lived in a small town; big city life was all he'd ever known. Everything about this new assignment would be unfamiliar. Was he ready for that?

As they joined Pastor Rob on the sidewalk, Peter took in the peeling white paint on the big old house. Half the lattice trim on the porch was missing. The front walk was cracked and buckling. Warped wooden steps led to the porch. Was the inside as bad as the exterior?

"An elderly couple, Cecil and Ida Brown, live here. Cecil had a stroke a few years ago, and he's never completely regained his speech or the use of his right side," Pastor Rob said.

"I'm certainly glad we can help them," Ashley said.

"Me, too. When Ida heard we were going to fix their house, she cried from happiness." Pastor Rob stopped in front of the steps and looked directly at Ashley. "I want you to let your father know how much we appreciate what he's doing for our community. I can't begin to explain what this project will mean to the folks you are helping. Many of them have lived in these houses all their lives. Their houses are falling down around them, and they have no resources to fix them."

"I'll be sure to tell him." Ashley's amber eyes shone with tears as they climbed the steps to the porch.

Peter realized the pastor's kind words about her father had touched her. He had the sudden urge to put an arm around her shoulders, but he squashed that thought before he could act on it. He had to maintain a certain distance from Ashley. She was a coworker on this project. He had to remember to treat this like an office situation, even without the four walls.

The floorboards of the porch squeaked as they approached the door. Before Pastor Rob could knock on the screen, the inside door opened.

A short, slightly stooped white-haired woman peered out at them. "Pastor Rob, did you bring me company?"

Motioning Peter and Ashley forward, Pastor Rob stepped aside. "Yes I did, Ida. How's Cecil today?"

"He's having a good day today. He's in the kitchen where I've been working."

Ida led them back to the kitchen, where Rob quickly made the introductions. Then Ida took them on a tour of the house. Peter made notes of the things that needed repair or paint. When they were done, Ida stopped in the kitchen. "Do y'all have time for some iced tea or lemonade and a little snack?"

"Certainly," Peter replied, then looked at Ashley as he suddenly remembered that he'd again made a decision without her input. How was he going to break himself of the habit? "Is that okay with you?"

"Sure." Her smile put his heart at ease.

Peter carried the tray from Ida containing glasses and the pitchers of iced tea and lemonade out to the porch. He set them on a small wooden table sitting in front of two wooden rockers and a porch swing. Ida followed closely behind carrying a plate filled with several kinds of crackers, while Pastor Rob assisted Cecil out to the porch and into his chair.

Ida set the plate on the table, then turned to Peter. "Thank you, young man. You remind me so much of our grandson. He lives down in Tampa, Florida. Too far away for me."

"You're welcome, Ida. What does your grandson do?"

"Oh, he works for some company. I can't remember the name, but he's doing very well in his job, and he has a sweet wife and a new baby boy." Ida motioned toward the rockers and the swing. "Y'all take a seat, and I'll serve."

Ashley stepped to the table. "We can serve ourselves."

Ida waved a hand at Ashley. "Nonsense. I don't mind serving you. It's one of the things I can still do these days. I like to feel useful." Ida turned and looked at Peter. "You have a seat on that swing with your young lady, and Pastor Rob and I'll take these rockers."

Peter didn't know how to respond to Ida's mistaken notion that he and Ashley had some kind of relationship other than work. Then he noticed Ashley's wide-eyed expression that told him she didn't know what to say either.

Following Ida's instructions without correcting her misperception was probably the easiest thing to do. He went over and sat on one end of the swing. He looked at Ashley and patted the space on the swing beside him. He couldn't help smiling as she traipsed over and sat next to him.

After Ida served everyone, she sat in the rocker and sipped her iced tea. Peter had opted for lemonade. He noticed Ashley had also taken lemonade. Was that something they had in common? Why was he searching for something to have in common with the young woman sitting next to him? He'd never before worried about things like that. Now it was constantly on his mind.

"When do you plan to start on Ida and Cecil's house?" Rob's words startled Peter from his thoughts.

That had been happening to him a lot lately, too. His mind often wandered off as he tried to figure out how he was going to fit into this whole mission thing—how he'd find a way to work with Ashley. As the bothersome thought zipped through his mind, he glanced at her. This time, he was going to check things out with her before he spoke. "What do you think, Ashley?"

When she looked at him, he could read the hint of panic in her eyes as she pushed up her glasses on her nose. "It's in the prospectus, right?"

Ah, yes, the prospectus, the one she hadn't read. Now he knew the reason for the panic. How ironic that consulting her made things worse. "Yes, the dates are in the prospectus. It's in the pickup. I'll go get it, so we can check them."

Peter hurried to the pickup and grabbed the prospectus from the portfolio. As he ambled back up the walk toward the house, he thumbed through the document to find the list of mission dates. A sense of relief washed over him when he came across the page that gave the details. The Browns' house was first on the list.

As he took his seat on the swing, he handed Ashley the prospectus with the page open to the list. She gave him a grateful smile, and his heart beat a little faster.

Taking a deep breath, he tried not to think about his reaction as he turned his attention to Ida and Cecil. "The third week in May is the date listed for work to begin on your house. The information shows that a group from a nearby college is going to spend the week with us." Peter leaned forward and patted Ida on the hand. "They'll get your house in A-1 shape."

Ida placed her other hand on top of Peter's, her gnarled fingers giving it a squeeze. "Cecil and I can't thank you enough."

"You're very welcome." Peter didn't feel as though his response was adequate, but he didn't know what else to say. Over the past two days, he'd had more feelings of inadequacy than he cared to think about. Until Ashley Hiatt had popped into his life, he had been a man who knew where he was going and what he wanted. Confidence was his middle name, or at least it had been.

Was God trying to tell him something?

Chapter Six

Ashley's heart turned over as Peter talked to Ida. She'd taken to him immediately, and he hadn't backed away. The Peter Dalton she remembered would never have spent time talking with an elderly woman. He'd been too busy escorting beautiful *young* women around town. Today, Ashley was seeing a much different side of Peter. She was realizing more and more that she might have misjudged him.

"Is there anything special I should do to get ready?" Ida asked.

"Be prepared to have lots of people in and out of your house." Peter patted her hand again, then handed her a piece of paper. "Here's the list of things I think we should fix. You and Cecil can look at it and tell me if there's anything I missed."

Smiling, Ida took the paper and shared it with her husband. Finally, she looked up at Peter. "This is so much more than I expected. I just thought you were going to paint our house."

"We're going to fix everything that's broken, so you won't have to worry."

"You're an answer to our prayers," Cecil said in his halting speech.

Tears welled in Ida's blue eyes. "Thank you. Thank you. You've covered everything. I can't thank you enough."

"It'll be our pleasure." Peter stood and looked at Ashley. "Do you think it's time we headed back to Atlanta?"

When Ashley heard Peter's stock phrase, she fought back a smile. At least that aspect of him was the same. Everything else he'd done today had surprised her. Besides winning the confidence of an elderly woman, he was asking for Ashley's opinion at every juncture, unlike his previous tendency to make decisions without consulting her. She'd asked to be involved in making the decisions, but now the problem lay with not always knowing the answers.

Looking at her watch, Ashley also stood. "Yes, we'd better head back."

When they bid goodbye to the Browns, Ashley observed the respect Peter gave the older couple. Ida, in turn, had succumbed to Peter's charm. Ashley mentally cautioned herself to be vigilant not to do the same. He was a very attractive and charismatic man. Falling for him would be too easy, especially since she was seeing a whole new, very likable side to him.

Ida and Cecil waved as their visitors left. While Peter was programming the GPS, a bouncy melody floated through the air. Ashley frowned. "What's that?"

Peter glanced around, then scooped Ashley's backpack from the console and held it up. "I believe the sound is coming from here. Could it possibly be your cell phone?"

Ashley snatched her backpack from Peter. "I don't know. I've never used it." She reached in and pulled out the cell phone. She shoved it at Peter. "You answer it, please."

He flipped it open and looked at the screen, then back at Ashley. "It's your father. Here."

Ashley took the phone. "Daddy?"

Her father's chuckle sounded in her ear. "What took you so long to answer?"

"I didn't realize it was my phone. We're just headed back to Atlanta."

"You can't leave yet. I'm on my way there."

"Why?"

"I'm taking you out to dinner."

"Where?"

"There's a restaurant right on the lake on the main road. Do you remember seeing it?"

"Yes."

"I'll meet you in about fifteen minutes."

"Okay." Ashley listened while her father gave her more details about the restaurant and recounted his day along with his decision to meet them and his plans for them. After he finished talking, Ashley said goodbye and flipped the phone closed. How was Peter going to take the news?

Peter put the GPS on the dash. "What did your father have to say?"

"He said we shouldn't leave, because he's only a few miles down the road. He wants to take us to dinner."

"Great!"

Peter's reply indicated excitement over her dad's arrival, but something in the set of his shoulders and the little wrinkle in his brow made Ashley think he wasn't as overjoyed with the prospect as his response indicated.

"Did he say why he's driving up here to meet us?" Peter asked.

"Yes, since we're here, he wants to talk about the mission project."

"I'm surprised he's making the trip, then turning around and going back in a few hours."

"That's just it. He's not going back."

"He's not? What's he planning to do?"

"He wants to spend the night and attend church here in the morning, and he'd like us to do the same."

Knitting his eyebrows, Peter frowned. "Are you prepared to do that?"

Ashley laughed. "Of course not. Neither of us is prepared, but that doesn't make any difference to Daddy. When he gets an idea in his head, it's full steam ahead."

Peter joined in the laughter. "Yeah, after working with him for fifteen years, I should know that."

"And someone else I know has a tendency to do the same thing, wouldn't you say?" She gave him a cheesy grin.

"Okay, you got me there."

"Daddy says we're supposed to stop at the local variety store before we meet him and buy what we need to spend the night. He said it's right here on Main Street. He told me church is pretty informal, so we don't have to worry about dressing up." She shrugged as she drove through the little town. "I know this probably wasn't in your plans."

"Yeah, but it gives me another chance to watch you do some speed shopping."

Ashley couldn't help laughing. "You mean you're not going to give me time to try on the clothes?"

"Hey, if you don't want to speed-shop, I'll give you all the time you want. I wouldn't want to get the blame if your clothes don't fit."

Ashley's stomach turned over when Peter winked at her. She gripped the steering wheel and focused her attention on the road. So many things about today had her liking Peter too much for her own good.

They entered the store, grabbed carts and went their separate ways. Ashley tried to make a mental list of the things she'd need. While she shopped, she kept glancing back toward the front of the store to see whether Peter had finished his shopping. Even though he said she could have as much time as she needed, she didn't want to keep him waiting.

Her competitive nature kicking into gear, she rushed through the narrow aisles and threw everything she needed into the cart. She tried on the clothes, then raced to the checkout. Peter was nowhere in sight. When she finally saw him coming toward her, she realized how silly she was acting again.

He smiled. "Hi. I see you beat me again."

"Yeah." Smiling sheepishly, she shrugged. "Put a shopping cart in my hands, and I can't help racing through the aisles."

Laughing, he held up a golf shirt and pair of twill pants. "Good thing the church service is casual. I'm going to look like I'm headed to the golf course rather than to church in these."

They made their purchases and hurried to the pickup. Driving toward the restaurant, Ashley thought about her father's impending visit. How was she going to deal with two men who had a tendency to plow ahead without any thought for the people around them? Was she creating a problem where none existed?

Her father and Peter were very successful businessmen. Maybe their decisiveness was what got things done, but she wasn't sure she could match their style. And she couldn't come close to matching their business knowledge. In some ways, she was out of her comfort zone and completely at their mercy. But she had to remember this was about God's work and not business.

The sun sat low in the sky just above the mountain peaks on the other side of the lake as Peter emerged from the pickup. He wasn't sure what to make of his boss's sudden appearance. Was he upset that Ashley and Peter had made this trip without telling him first, or was Richard making sure his daughter had survived the drive? For a dozen years, Peter had had his boss's complete confidence. Was that still the case?

Richard approached them from across the restaurant parking lot. "I see you found the place."

"Hi, Daddy. I'm so surprised you came up." Ashley raced to meet her father and gave him a big hug.

Richard draped an arm around Ashley's shoulders as they walked leisurely toward the restaurant entrance.

Peter lagged behind, feeling like an outsider as he watched them. He had to get beyond his disappointment over being shuffled off to the boonies. He'd seen for himself today that people like the Browns needed help, so he was going to do his best to help them, no matter what the reason—pleasing his boss or pleasing Ashley. Or maybe he was finally seeing this assignment as pleasing God. He needed an attitude adjustment, and that was what he intended to work on tonight and in the weeks to come.

When Ashley reached the door, Richard opened it for her. Before she stepped inside, she turned and looked at Peter. "You're being very slow."

"Just taking in the scenery." Peter smiled wryly as he jogged to catch up. "Besides, I had to catch my breath after the speed shopping."

She gave him a wry smile and pushed up her glasses, then looked past him. "I've forgotten how picturesque the mountains are. The sunset's going to be beautiful."

"You've got that right." *Just as beautiful as you.* The unexpected thought threw him another curve. What was he thinking? She wasn't as striking as the women he'd dated over the years, but she was beautiful inside. There was a vitality about her— an inner loveliness that made her beautiful.

Maybe that had always been his problem with women. He hadn't concentrated on the inner beauty that was lasting. But he didn't need to be thinking about Ashley Hiatt in the context of attractiveness. How many times did he have to remind himself that she was the boss's daughter and off-limits in so many ways?

Lively conversation and the clinking sound of glassware

and utensils floated toward the hostess stand where they stopped. Although the restaurant was relatively busy, they didn't have to wait. When the hostess showed them to a table, Ashley took a chair and Richard sat beside her. Peter took his place opposite them. For a few minutes, they silently studied their menus.

Richard closed his menu and placed it on the table. "First, I have to say how excited I am that y'all decided to make the trip up here. I was worried one or the other of you wouldn't agree to this project, especially after I dumped it in your laps without warning. Can I take it that you're both on board with the mission?"

Glancing at Ashley, Peter waited for her to answer first.

She slipped an arm through her father's. "Yes, Daddy, I'm on board." Then she looked over at Peter.

Her scrutiny made his heart race. He swallowed hard. "Me, too, sir."

There. He'd said it. He'd made his commitment. Never in his life had he imagined himself in this position. Would he be good at this mission stuff? He'd always managed fine in the business world. But this wasn't just business. It was God's work, not his.

"Terrific!" Richard put an arm around Ashley's shoulders and pulled her close. Then he reached across the table to shake Peter's hand. "You've made me a very happy man. Now tell me about your day. How'd my girl do driving her pickup?"

After Richard threw out the question, Peter glanced at Ashley. No irritation showed on her face, but how did she feel about having to report on her driving? He was going to give Richard a glowing report. She deserved it after putting up with the ridiculous exercise. "Richard, you have nothing to worry about. Ashley is a very competent driver."

Ashley flashed Peter a grateful smile. "Thanks, Peter." She

turned her attention to her father. "See. I told you I didn't need driving lessons."

Richard sighed. "I wanted to be sure you could handle the pickup."

"I guess I understand, but you did embarrass me."

"Forgive your old dad for wanting to keep you safe?"

"You're forgiven, especially since I love the pickup. I feel like I own the road when I'm driving it. It's a whole lot different driving a big vehicle than a small car."

"Well, don't get to owning the road too much. There are other cars out there, too." Richard smiled indulgently at her.

Shaking her head, Ashley gave her dad a playful punch on the arm. "Don't tease me."

The waitress appeared and took their order. As soon as she left, Ashley launched into a detailed report about their meeting with the pastor and other church members, their proposed living arrangements and their visit with Ida and Cecil. Peter sat back and let her do the talking. He was enjoying the vitality he'd seen in her earlier. Her excitement was contagious.

Richard turned his attention to Peter. "I'm not hearing anything from you."

"Ashley covered it all." Peter shook his head. "I don't have anything to add. I'm just ready to get started."

"When do you plan to move here?"

"Good question. I know the Cummingses and the Weavers said they were ready to have us move in as soon as we wanted." Peter glanced at Ashley. "What do you think?"

Rather than answer him, she turned to her father. "What preparations do we need to make before we do the first house?"

"Buy the supplies. I've already negotiated a good deal with a local building supply. They're going to give us a very good discount on paint, lumber and whatever else we need."

"Great," Peter said. "In the prospectus, you listed the houses we'll be renovating. We saw one of those today, and I see one problem."

"What's that?" Richard asked.

"Most likely our volunteers won't be able to do the plumbing repairs and electrical work. What do we do with those kinds of things?" Peter hoped he hadn't missed something in the prospectus that dealt with those issues. "I can do a little electrical work, but not plumbing."

"If the volunteers can't handle the work, we'll hire that work out. I've compiled a list of contractors in the area." Richard reached for his jacket, pulled a piece of paper out of one pocket and handed it to Peter.

"Thanks. I know we'll need some of these people for the Browns' house. It'll take way more than paint to get that house in shape."

As Peter pocketed the list, the waitress brought their food. Steam rose from the dishes, and delicious smells wafted around their table. After the waitress left, Richard looked at Ashley. "Would you like to give the blessing?"

"Sure."

Bowing his head, Peter breathed a sigh of relief that Richard hadn't asked him to pray again. Peter planned to work on his own private prayer time, but this praying aloud was not in his comfort zone. Fortunately, fixing houses was.

He listened to Ashley's sweet voice praising God for His goodness and guidance in allowing them to share their blessings with those who were less fortunate. After she said the final *amen*, he started to eat, realizing how truly blessed his life had been. He needed to see even his new role as a blessing, not a derailment of his career. Convincing himself of that fact wasn't going to be easy.

While they ate, Richard told them about his golf game. Then the conversation turned again to the upcoming work. They made plans to order supplies for the renovations and to move the following week. Richard also mentioned the office space he'd rented and suggested they look at it after they ate.

As the conversation waned, Ashley eyed her father. "Daddy, exactly what did you plan to do before I was suddenly forced to come home from the mission? Who was going to run this operation? Just Peter?"

Richard cut a piece of his steak and popped it into his mouth as if to avoid answering. Peter had to hand it to Ashley. She knew how to put her father on the spot. Peter decided he should keep her tendency to ask tough questions in mind while he worked with her. He was as eager as Ashley to hear Richard's answer. Then maybe he would understand why his boss had chosen him instead of someone else to do this work.

Finally, Richard set his knife and fork on his plate and leaned back. He took a deep breath and let it out slowly. "You know, it was over a year ago that God put this project on my heart. I've never been one to think a lot about God's specific leading, but the idea came to mind, and it wouldn't let me go."

"You know, sometimes, God really does work like that." Ashley smiled at her father.

"I'm beginning to realize that, sugar. Anyway, I prayed for workers." Richard held out his hands. "And God sent you."

"So you believe my coming home was an answer to your prayer?"

"Absolutely." He gave her a wink. "What do you think?"

"I'm beginning to see that, too, although I still have a problem seeing how God can work through all the trouble I left behind."

Richard gave her shoulders another squeeze. "I agree. Sometimes it's hard to see how God can use such evil for good."

Listening to the exchange, Peter wondered how he fit into this prayer. He hadn't been called from anything except a great job he loved. But he couldn't voice his question without leaving the impression he wasn't on board with the project. Besides, it would make him look like he was only thinking about himself. Maybe he was. If only Ashley would ask the question for him.

Ashley glanced Peter's way. Then, as if she could read his mind, she looked at her father. "So why did you pick Peter to work on this project?"

For an instant, Peter wanted to slip underneath the table. He'd wanted to ask that question, but now that it was out there waiting for an answer, he wasn't sure he wanted to know. Ashley knew how to put everyone on the spot, not just her father.

Richard chuckled. "You know, I'm glad you asked that question, sugar, because Peter needs to know why I chose him. It's something I should've said the other night, when I first brought this up."

Peter held his breath while he waited for Richard to finally make his point.

"Peter, you've been one of my best employees. I could always count on you to do the job and get it done right."

"Thank you, sir. And you've rewarded me greatly."

"I'm glad to show my appreciation for work well done."

Despite Richard's obvious praise, Peter wondered how being pushed out of his position to work on this project was a reward, but he certainly wasn't going to ask. "It's been my pleasure to work for you all these years."

"I've always been glad I decided to hire you and then promote you over the years. I wanted to see this mission project run well, and I couldn't think of anyone better than you to run it."

"Thank you, sir, for your confidence in me."

"With your business sense and Ashley's mission experience, I know this project will be in excellent hands."

"We'll do our best, sir."

As they finished their meal, Peter's heart was a little lighter, knowing his boss had chosen him because he wanted the best for this project. He should be honored, but he couldn't help thinking about the coveted position that would never be his— the head of Hiatt Construction.

After they left the restaurant, Peter and Ashley followed Richard over to the rented office space, a brick-front building that appeared to have housed some kind of business at one time. He unlocked the door and flipped the light switch. Peter blinked as the overhead fluorescents illuminated the space.

"Well, what do you think?" Richard asked.

Hoping Ashley would answer first, Peter didn't say a thing. What could he say about an empty room? He tried to imagine working side by side with Ashley here. He tried to picture his life in this small town. He tried not to have a pessimistic attitude, but all of his thoughts came up negative. He felt good about this mission one minute and troubled the next. Was this where the prayer part came in—the part he hadn't bothered to pursue?

Ashley wandered around the room, looking inside cupboards and closets. "It's nice and clean and ready for us to move in, but what about office furniture and stuff like that?"

"That's all been ordered. I'll arrange to have it delivered, so it'll be here as soon as you arrive."

Ashley stood in the middle of the room and held out her arms. "I've never had an office before. I think it's perfect. What do you think, Peter?"

She'd put him on the spot again. He had warned himself about her tendency to do that. If only he could generate some of her enthusiasm about this office space for himself. Sometimes she reminded him of Pollyanna with her happy-face attitude. "Sure. It's very serviceable."

Ashley frowned at him. "Only serviceable? Look out this big window. How can you not love the fabulous view of the mountains?"

"Yeah, the view's great."

"You don't sound very excited about it." Ashley moved over to the window and looked out. "You can see God's handiwork every day when you look out."

"Good thought." Peter wanted to frown, but he forced a smile and hoped Richard wouldn't think he was ungrateful for the office space. What had happened to the girl who couldn't see eye-to-eye with her father on anything?

He'd seen a glimpse of her that first evening when Richard announced his plans, but now, Ashley seemed in agreement with whatever her father did. Was her change in attitude a result of the praying she'd done? He had a lot to learn—not about missions but about letting God change his point of view.

Chapter Seven

Turning from the window, Ashley glanced at Peter. He didn't seem very happy. She should never have questioned his assessment of the office. Changing the subject was a good idea. "Daddy, where do you plan to stay tonight?"

"I'm thinking about buying property in this area. I found a house on the lake for sale, and I've rented it for tonight. There's plenty of room, so we can all stay there."

Ashley's heart sank. "Are you planning to sell the house in Atlanta?"

"No, I thought it might be nice to have a vacation place up here in the mountains. And there's a golf course nearby, so I can golf when I come up."

"You're always working. When will you have time to use it?" Ashley asked, wondering what had prompted her father to look into vacation homes. This concern about eating right, watching his weight and doing missions wasn't like him at all. Was there something going on in his life that he wasn't telling her? Was he not being honest about his health? She wanted to ask, but not in front of Peter.

"If I decide to purchase it, I'll make the time to use it. Let's head out there now."

"Okay. Lead the way."

Driving through the quiet streets, Ashley followed her father out of town. Peter had opted to ride with her father because he wanted to discuss the mission funds. Despite the nice things she'd discovered about him today, she also realized they came at life from different perspectives. Business was his middle name, and he didn't care about the view from the office window. Could *she* think like a businessperson, or at least, think with that perspective in mind? Working with him every day would require it.

When they arrived at the rental house nestled amongst the trees on a lakefront lot, Ashley took in the beauty of the darkened sky dotted with stars. Beyond the log house, the lake glistened in the moonlight. Everything here testified to the wonder of God's creation.

Once they were inside, her father turned to her. "Well, what do you think?"

Her father had said those exact words to her when they'd looked at the office. Despite the closed-up, musty smell that greeted them, she immediately wanted to gush over the fabulous view of the lake through the wall of windows at the back of the house, but she hesitated. Would Peter dismiss her joy over the magnificent view?

Why did she care what Peter thought? This wasn't about business. This was about her father's wish to find a relaxing retreat. She marched to the windows and gazed out. "It really doesn't matter what I think. You have to like it, not me."

"True, but I'd still like your opinion. Let's take a better look out here on the deck."

"Okay." Ashley followed her father onto the deck running the length of the house and overlooking the tree-covered hillside and the lake below. She leaned on the balustrade. "It's really breathtaking, Daddy."

Peter joined them on the deck. "Now this is a view I can get excited about."

Ashley turned to look at him. Even in the moonlight she could read the awe radiating from his eyes. Surprised at his reaction, she motioned toward the house. "Maybe Daddy should buy this place and put the office here."

Peter laughed. "No, then I wouldn't get any work done. I'd be gazing at the lake all day. Offices don't need a view. They're for working."

"You're probably right." So that was the reason for his blasé comment about the view at the office. Slowly, she was beginning to understand Peter, or she hoped that was the case. Insight was key to a good working relationship.

Richard turned to go inside. "Let's look at the rest of the place."

As they toured the house, Richard checked out everything with the practiced eye of an experienced builder. He and Peter discussed the superior workmanship that was apparent throughout the house. After they determined where everyone would sleep, they returned to the deck and made themselves comfortable on the wooden rockers.

Peter and Richard continued discussing the details of the house out on the deck. While they shared their knowledge of good construction, a tinge of jealousy pricked at Ashley's heart. She shouldn't begrudge her father the male companionship that Peter afforded. He was probably like a son and shared many of her father's interests. Because she'd never shown an interest in her father's business, she couldn't fault them for leaving her out of the conversation.

Finally, her father stood and stretched his arms above his head. "I'm going to call it a night. I'll see you two in the morning. Church is at ten."

"Okay, Daddy." Ashley went over and gave her dad a kiss on the cheek.

After her father left, Ashley walked to the balustrade and wondered whether she should excuse herself, too. Would it be rude to leave Peter by himself? She didn't know how to act around him. When would she feel at ease in his presence?

There was always this strange tension brewing just below the surface of their conversations and interactions. She couldn't quite figure out her response. She'd been prepared not to like him, but that wasn't a Christian attitude. Then her determination to accept him opened up some feelings she wasn't prepared to acknowledge.

Peter joined her. "Your dad's excited about this project."

"Yeah," she replied, seeing no chance to escape since Peter wanted to talk. "And I think he kind of likes this house."

"It's a great place. I wouldn't mind having a place like this myself."

"Where do you live now?"

"I have a condo in Alpharetta." He laughed halfheartedly. "But I'll be trading my condo for a room at the pastor's house."

"And how do you feel about that?"

"I haven't had time to digest it. I just went with it because I wanted to please your dad. He's been a great mentor and his approval means a lot to me."

Surprised at Peter's admission, Ashley found another thing to like about him. He was giving up a lot to please her father. What was his motivation? She wished he wouldn't keep her off balance all of the time. "Thank you for that."

"You're welcome. I have a lot of respect for your father."

Ashley didn't know what to say. His statements made her wonder whether he was saying this stuff to get on her good side and have the boss's daughter put in a good word for him. Why did she always have to doubt the sincerity of his words or his intentions? What made her so skeptical?

She didn't really know him that well, and the judgments she'd formed were from observations she'd made years ago. She needed to let go of old perceptions. She should leave the judging to God. "My dad's a wonderful man, but I didn't always appreciate him when I was growing up."

"Do any of us appreciate our parents when we're kids?"

"Are you saying you didn't appreciate your parents?"

He chuckled. "Yeah, I guess that's what I'm saying. I think it takes being an adult to value our parents."

"I think I'm still learning that lesson."

"Yeah, we do need to keep learning our whole lives." Peter yawned. "And after those rather philosophical words of wisdom, I'm also calling it a night. See you in the morning."

"Sure. Good night." Ashley kept her gaze trained on the lake as Peter left. She couldn't believe she'd admitted to him that she was still learning to value her father's advice. Peter probably thought she was an ungrateful child because she hadn't been interested in her father's business.

She couldn't worry about how Peter viewed her. The more important thing right now was showing her father that she cared. Wasn't that part of the reason she'd decided to do this mission? So she wasn't much different than Peter. They both wanted to please her father.

The steeple on the old brick church building rose into the clear blue sky. Glad she'd purchased a sweater for the cool April morning, Ashley stood on the front walk while Peter and her father talked with several men following the church service.

Despite the traditional look of the building and the sanctuary with its dark pews and matching woodwork, the congregation had a contemporary worship service with a praise band. Ashley had enjoyed it, but Peter had seemed uneasy as he sat next to her in the pew.

While she stood there speculating about Peter's reaction to the church service, two teenage girls ran up to her. One had bright blue eyes and thick, medium-brown hair swishing around her shoulders. The other sported a short, curly cut for her lighter brown hair. Her gray eyes beamed as she gazed at Ashley.

The taller girl with short hair skidded to a stop in front of her. "Hi, are you Ashley Hiatt?"

"Yes."

"Our mom, Teresa Weaver, said she met you yesterday. So we wanted to introduce ourselves. I'm Jessica and this is my sister, Libby. We're so excited you're going to stay with us."

"I'm glad to meet you."

"We were wondering when you plan to move in," Libby said.

"Sometime next week. I'm going to let your mom know the exact day after I get back to Atlanta and see how everything plays out. Peter Dalton will be working with me and staying with Pastor Cummings. We have to coordinate everything."

The girls giggled as they whispered behind their hands. "Is Peter Dalton that stiff, formal dude over there?" Jessica nodded her head toward Peter. "Have you ever seen anyone with such perfect hair? Not a strand out of place."

Ashley pinched her lips together to keep from joining in their giggles. Finally, she gained control and managed a smile. "If you mean the tall guy in the green polo shirt and tan khakis, then, yes."

In tandem, the girls giggled again. Then Jessica grimaced. "Sorry. We didn't mean to make fun. You won't tell him what we said, will you?"

Ashley chuckled, knowing she wouldn't even consider telling him. "I won't. Besides, he wouldn't care. He's a very nice man."

"Thank you." Libby placed a hand over her heart. "Our mom already asked your dad to stay and have lunch with us. So we'll see you back at our place."

"Okay." Ashley waved as the girls walked away.

While Ashley waited for the men to finish conversing, she tried to look at Peter through the eyes of a teenage girl. Stiff. Formal. Perfect hair. Did that describe him?

At the moment, not one strand of his sandy brown hair *was* out place. Ashley could see the description fitting him, if you didn't know him. In fact, wasn't that the way she'd seen him when she was a teenager? Now she saw him as a capable businessman with a dash of compassion.

He wasn't completely hard-nosed. He'd proven that yesterday when he gave her the key chain. Then at lunch, he'd attempted to explain away his statement about not wanting to get on her bad side. In his frustration, he'd run his hand through his hair and made it very messy. He'd been kind of cute with his messy hair. That was a dangerous thought—a slippery slope to liking Peter Dalton way more than she should.

After the men finished their conversation, they headed to Richard's car. Riding alone in her pickup to the Weavers' house, Ashley examined her disappointment that Peter wasn't riding with her. She shouldn't make this personal. For Peter, this was about pleasing her father. Isn't that what he'd said last night?

When they reached the Weavers' house, Ashley parked behind her father's car. She walked between them as they went up the front walk. Before they reached the porch, Jessica and Libby bounded out the front door. They immediately began talking over each other in their excitement as they grabbed Ashley and escorted her into the big rambling house. She wished she could see her dad's and Peter's expressions.

Once inside, Jessica and Libby stopped at the foot of the staircase near the front door. "We want to show you your room. We hope you like it."

Ashley followed them up the stairs while they talked a mile a minute. At the top of the stairs, the girls stopped and turned down the hallway to the left, where a multicolored runner covered the hardwood floors.

Libby stopped at the first door on the right. "This is the bathroom. We have to share. I hope that's okay with you." Before Ashley could comment, Libby babbled on, "And your room is the next door on the right across the hall from mine. It used to belong to my oldest brother, but when he got married Mom made it into her sewing room. Now she's fixed it up for you. We helped."

Jessica swung the door open. Ashley glanced inside. A mahogany sleigh bed, matching chest and nightstand filled the room. A patchwork quilt lay across the bed, and an oval braided rug in matching colors sat on the floor next to the bed.

"What a lovely room!" Ashley said.

"I'm so glad you like it. The furniture used to be our grandma's. She made the quilt." Jessica pulled Ashley farther into the room. "And your room looks out over the backyard."

"Your grandma is very talented." Ashley went over to the window and looked out. A white picket fence enclosed the backyard. Should she have expected anything else? Smoke curled upward from a grill on the patio. "This is great."

"We can hardly wait till you move in." Libby showed Ashley the closet and opened every drawer in the chest. "I hope there's room for all your stuff."

"There's plenty of room." If only they knew how little she had. Being on the mission field had made her realize she didn't need a lot. Since her return, she'd been dragged back into the culture of too many things.

As much as she looked forward to sharing the next few months with the two lively teenagers, she suddenly felt overwhelmed by their constant chatter. She wondered which girl talked more. Was she ready to live with this family?

Even though she'd lived with a missionary family while she

was in Africa, she'd maintained a fairly separate life. She always felt they needed their own family time without her presence. Now she was going to be thrust right into the middle of this family. Was she ready? Were they?

Doubts swirled in her mind like the smoke swirling above the grill outside, but she pushed every one of them aside.

After the meal, Peter stood beside the pickup while Ashley said goodbye to Jessica and Libby. How was she going to survive with those chatterboxes? Maybe everything would work out fine. The two teens would talk, and Ashley would listen.

With a final wave, she approached the pickup. "You're riding back with me?"

"Yeah. Why wouldn't I?"

"Because you've been riding everywhere with Daddy since he showed up."

"That's because we had things to discuss."

"And you don't have anything more to talk about?"

"No."

"Are you sure?" Ashley narrowed her gaze. "Or did Daddy tell you to ride back with me, so you can keep an eye on me?"

Peter couldn't help laughing. "You are a suspicious woman."

"Yes, and you haven't answered my question."

"Your dad isn't spying." Peter winked at her. "I just have this policy of going home with the girl I came with."

Grabbing her keys from her backpack, she marched around the pickup and opened the driver's side door. "Well, you don't have to ride with me if you don't want to. Don't feel obligated."

"I'm not feeling obligated." Getting into the pickup, Peter was tempted to laugh again, but he refrained. What had made her all huffy? He was only trying to make a joke. As long as he lived, he was sure he'd never understand women, especially this woman. "Would you like me to program the GPS?"

"Yes, please."

"I have some things I need to talk over with you."

Ashley glanced at him as she turned the key and the engine roared to life. "You do?"

"Sure. I know we made tentative plans about moving up here, but I wanted to nail everything down. Is that okay with you?"

"Yes." She pulled the pickup into the street. "I'm sorry if I'm being oversensitive to Daddy's hovering."

Peter felt free to laugh at her statement this time. "I understand, but cut him some slack. He wants the best for you because he loves you."

"I know, but he doesn't have to smother me."

"Look at it this way. In a few days you'll be living here, not with your dad."

"Yeah, but what if he buys that house?"

"He still has a company to run."

"But he said he'd find the time to make it up here."

"True, but real estate transactions don't happen overnight. You're safe for a few weeks." Peter had some reasons of his own for worrying about Richard's quest for vacation property. Did his search mean that he was considering an early retirement?

Richard's early retirement would mean someone stepping into his shoes to run the company. Despite the signs to the contrary, Peter still hoped that he would be that someone. But taking on this mission job dimmed his hopes for getting that position. Why couldn't he let his dream die? Because giving up wasn't in his nature.

"I hope you're right about the time it takes to purchase a piece of property."

"Even the quickest transactions require inspections and time for attorneys to draw up the documents for the closing."

"Okay, you've convinced me that it won't happen overnight, but I'm sure it'll happen before the summer's over."

"That's possible."

Ashley didn't say anything for a few minutes as she made her way out of town on the main road. After she'd driven several miles, she sighed loudly. "I suppose you think I'm pretty awful for not wanting my dad nearby."

How did he answer that loaded question? If he said yes, then she'd think *he* was awful. Was it possible to come up with a diplomatic answer? He weighed his words carefully. "I can understand not wanting to have your dad managing your life. My mother does a good job of hovering, so I can sympathize."

"Thanks." Smiling, Ashley glanced at him. "I love my dad, and I do want to please him, but I want him to realize I can make my own decisions. What's so odd is when I was growing up he encouraged me to be my own person. But when I was old enough to go out on my own, he was suddenly upset when I chose to do something different than what he'd planned."

Peter recognized Ashley's plight from the conversation he'd had with Charlotte. "We have at least one thing in common. We both want to please your dad."

"Do you think that's the only thing we have in common?"

"I don't know. You tell me." Here she was again, putting him on the spot. She could certainly cut to the chase. He would have to get used to her forthright way of dealing with things. At least her directness would always let him know where he stood.

"That's something we'll have to figure out when we get to know each other better."

"We'll have the rest of the spring and the whole summer to do that."

"Yeah." Would they get to know each other by then, or would they remain the boss's go-to guy and the boss's daughter?

She'd only been back for a few days, yet it seemed as though she'd been here much longer. He couldn't quite figure out why he felt that way. Despite her candor, there was so much about her that he couldn't pin down.

"Now that we've discussed dealing with my dad, what did you want to discuss about the move?" She continued to look straight ahead.

"You said you were ready to move on Tuesday. That's the day after tomorrow."

"I'm aware of what day it is." She sighed. "I'm sorry. I didn't mean to be so sharp."

"No problem. It's been a long weekend. I want to be sure you'll be ready. You've only been home a couple of days, and I didn't know whether you had enough time to pack your things."

"I don't have a lot to pack, do you?"

Under no circumstances did Peter want to admit that he had more stuff to pack than a woman. But Ashley wasn't just any woman. He was fast learning that. "No. If you can be ready on Tuesday, so can I. Do you want to travel together?"

"Sure."

"Okay." Why did her response please him so much? He didn't want to examine the question too closely. He might find the answer unsettling. "We can meet at my place, so I won't have to backtrack."

"That works. Remind me to have you program your address into the GPS when we get back."

"I'll make a note of that. Let's discuss our plans for Ida and Cecil's house. I want everything in place when we start."

"Yes, sir." She gave him a little salute.

Peter grabbed a pen and a legal pad from his portfolio. He hoped her gesture didn't mean she thought he was ordering her around. For the rest of the trip, they made plans and Peter took notes.

When Ashley stopped at her house, the trees lining the drive cast long shadows in the late afternoon sun. She punched the button on the remote, and the garage door went up.

After she drove into the garage, Peter programmed his address into the GPS unit, then turned it off. "There. You're set for our next trip up north."

"There. I got you back in one piece, and I didn't even crash into the wall when I drove into the garage." Smiling, she glanced his way. "Thanks for indulging my dad by being my driving instructor."

"I'll be your driving instructor any time you want." Although he'd jokingly made the remark, he realized he actually meant it. He'd enjoyed their time together. She kept him on his toes, but that was part of the fun.

"No offense, but I hope my dad doesn't request any more driving lessons for me." She opened the door. "Would you like to come in before you head home?"

Glad for the invitation, Peter smiled. "I can only stay for a few minutes, but I'll help you bring in your stuff. Then I have to head off to my parents' place."

"If you have to go, I can get this stuff inside by myself."

Peter studied Ashley as she picked up a couple of bags from the backseat. Did he detect a little disappointment in the tone of her voice—disappointment that he couldn't stay longer? No doubt it was just his ego reaching for something that wasn't there. He grabbed the remaining bags. "I've got time to help. I'm not in that big of a rush."

As he followed Ashley into the house, he still wondered about his motivations. Was he doing this to please his boss or to please Ashley? He wanted to stay on Richard's good side, but he also had a fascination with Ashley that he couldn't quite wrap his mind around. She was like a challenging jigsaw puzzle: He wanted to fit all of the pieces together and get the whole picture.

The past two days with her had taught him that he had a lot to learn—about missions and about Ashley. He still wasn't sure what had possessed him to buy her the key chain. She probably had enough money to buy and sell him three times over, but she didn't care about any of it.

Maybe he'd wanted her to have something because she always thought of others rather than herself. She could teach him a lot about helping others. Without even knowing her influence on him, she'd already taught him how to give.

Ashley set her packages on the built-in desk in the kitchen. "I'm so sorry I almost dismissed Daddy's desire to fund this project. Your willingness to participate made me realize its importance. You showed me the way. Thank you."

"You're very welcome, but I didn't do anything." He was showing her the way? If she only knew how laughable her assessment was, she'd turn him in for being a fraud. Now he was determined to live up to her opinion.

Chapter Eight

Peter arrived at his parents' home just before six o'clock. How would they feel about his impending move? What would they say about his new position? He had a bad feeling about their reaction.

He let himself into the house through the back door that led from the screened porch into the kitchen. Gloria Dalton stood in front of the sink while she scrubbed a potato with a vegetable brush. Mouthwatering smells wafted through the room.

"Hey, Mom. What's cooking? Got enough to feed one more?"

She turned from the sink and wiped her hands on a nearby towel. "Peter, what a nice surprise! We're having meatloaf, and I think I can manage to find another potato."

"Great. Sounds delicious. I haven't had your meatloaf in ages." He walked over and gave her a hug.

"What brings you by? And where have you been all weekend? I've been trying to reach you. You didn't answer your cell phone, and I didn't see you in church this morning."

"I've been busy." He'd deliberately not responded to his mother's calls because this job change was something he wanted to tell his parents about in person. "What did you want?"

"I wanted to discuss the plans we made at Matt and Rachel's wedding for the family get-together."

Peter rubbed the back of his neck. He'd forgotten about that. Now what was he supposed to do? "Mom, I can't go."

"Why not? That'll ruin everything. We wanted you three boys to be there. Matt and Wade have already agreed, and you were all for it at the wedding."

"That was before Richard put me in charge of this new project. It can't be helped."

"You can't let your job own you. You need to take time off."

"This is something different. That's why I stopped by. I have some news."

Gloria clasped her hands together. "You've finally found the right girl to marry."

"No, Mom. Nothing like that." She was always pushing for him to find a wife, but she never liked any of the women he dated. That was fine with him because eventually he didn't like them, either. He shook his head even as a fleeting image of Ashley crossed his mind. Sure, she was intriguing, but they hardly knew each other, and she wasn't his type.

"Then what is it?"

"Can it wait until Dad's here?"

"Peter, you can't leave me hanging like this."

"You'll survive until then."

"At least tell me this isn't something bad."

"It's nothing for you to worry about."

"Then why the secrecy?"

"There's no secret. I just want to tell you both at the same time."

"Is this just an excuse to get you a home-cooked meal?"

"Maybe." Peter laughed. "Do you need help with dinner?"

"Find another potato. There should be one in the vegetable bin. Then you can set the table."

As Peter was setting the table, Harold Dalton walked into the kitchen. "Hey, Dad."

Harold gave his wife a peck on the cheek, then walked over and clapped Peter on the back. "I'm glad you stopped by. Your mother's been having a fit because she couldn't get a hold of you all weekend. She's determined to have this big family thing this summer, and she wants to get everything in place now."

Releasing a heavy sigh, Peter put the last piece of flatware on the table, then turned to his dad. "And I'm going to ruin it all."

Harold frowned. "How's that?"

The timer on the microwave sounded, and Gloria opened the door and put the baked potatoes in a bowl. "Peter, don't tell him while I'm trying to get dinner on the table. Here, take these to the table, and your dad and I will get the rest. You can tell us when we're seated."

Peter shook his head as he placed the bowl of potatoes on the table. First, his mom couldn't wait to find out. Now she was making him wait to make his announcement.

After they were seated, Harold said a blessing. Peter prayed that they'd be receptive to his new position.

His mom handed him the meatloaf. "So what's your news?"

Peter took a deep breath and let it out slowly. "I'm moving because—"

"Moving? Why are you moving? Where are you moving?" Gloria's fork dropped onto her plate, the clang sounding an ominous note across the table. "You can't move. It's bad enough with Matt living halfway across the country and Wade living in Florida without you moving, too."

"Gloria, let Peter explain."

Peter glanced from one parent to the other. "It's not a permanent move. Just from now through the summer."

"Why would you move just for the summer?" she asked.

Harold patted his wife's hand. "Let him finish."

"I've got a new job." Peter waited for his statement to register before he continued. "I'm moving to a little town up in the north Georgia mountains on Tuesday."

"So soon? You've quit at Hiatt Construction? How could you have a better position than the one you have with Hiatt? What kind of job would take you up there?" Gloria peppered the air with her questions.

Peter crossed his arms and settled back in his chair as he gazed at his mother. "Do you remember my saying Richard has put me on a new project?"

"Oh, yes. I remember."

"So are you building a new resort up there?"

"No, I'm doing mission work." Peter took in his parents' puzzled expressions.

"What does mission work have to do with Hiatt Construction?" Harold asked.

"Here's the deal." Peter hurriedly explained Richard's plan and how Peter and Ashley would be working together.

"Ashley Hiatt. I thought she was teaching missionaries' children in Africa." Gloria took a sip of her iced tea.

"She was until about a week ago." With Ashley's image running around in his head, Peter explained the circumstances surrounding her return.

"What a frightening experience for her! How do you feel about working with the boss's daughter?" Gloria asked.

"It shouldn't be any different than working with anyone else." Peter tried to convince himself that his statement was true. Working with Ashley wasn't his main concern. His main concern was how often thoughts of her came unbidden to his mind. Maybe it was only natural that he would think about her because they'd spent nearly the entire weekend in each other's company.

Thinking about her wasn't the problem. The problem was *how* he was thinking about her. He remembered how she wrinkled her nose when she was thinking hard, how she liked to speed-shop, how she wasn't afraid to ask a tough question and how she cared about people. He feared that in such a short time, she was making him like her too much.

With his less-than-dedicated spiritual life, what business did he have letting himself even consider Ashley in a romantic sense? Besides, hadn't he decided long ago that serious relationships only caused trouble?

"This is very admirable work, but what happens at the end of the summer?" His mother's question snapped him from his worrisome thoughts.

"That's something Ashley and I will develop. Richard got this first phase started, and we'll carry on from there. Summer's a good time for youth groups, church groups and families on vacation to do short-term mission projects. This program helps facilitate their desire to help."

Gloria sat forward and grinned as she clasped her hands together. "I have a fabulous idea. We'll have the family get together up in the mountains this summer. What do you think?"

Peter didn't dare squash the eagerness he heard in his mother's voice. Besides, her acceptance made his heart lighter. As he took a bite of meatloaf, he could already see the wheels spinning in her mind. "If you think you can work it out, your plan sounds fine to me."

Harold set his fork on his plate and gazed at his wife. "Are you intending to join in the project?"

"Of course."

"What about the children? Aren't they too young to partic-ipate?" Harold asked.

Gloria's smile disappeared. "What do you think, Peter?"

"The littlest ones, Jack and Danny, are too young. But I'm sure there's something we can find for the three school-aged girls to do. Let's see whether everyone will agree to do this before we worry about what to do with the kids. Of course, there's always the option of Grandma Gloria riding herd on the group."

"Peter, you're so smart." Gloria smiled.

"I get all my brains from my parents."

His mother pretended to look perturbed. "Don't try to flatter us."

"You mean flattery won't get me anywhere?"

"It might get you some of my apple crisp."

"With ice cream?"

Gloria laughed. "Now you sound like one of the kids."

"I'm a kid at heart."

Chuckling, Harold shook his head. "Peter, you haven't been a kid at heart since you were ten. You were too serious. If it hadn't been for your brothers, you would've had your nose buried in a book all of the time. I think this project is going to be good for you. It'll be a great change from the pressure-filled work you've been doing at Hiatt Construction."

Peter cut a bite of potato. "It may be a different kind of pressure—the pressure of dealing with a completely foreign situation. I wonder whether I know what I'm doing."

"I have no doubt you'll be successful, and you'll be working in a more relaxed atmosphere," Harold said.

"We'll see." Peter resumed eating.

His parents had always been supportive of every endeavor he'd undertaken, whether it was his attempt to build a tree house in the backyard or manage the construction of a sky-scraper. At this point, building this mission project seemed almost as intimidating as building a skyscraper. But he was going to make certain this project was a success.

Ashley surveyed the room filled with new desks, computers, copiers and everything an efficient office demanded. Her father had spared no expense in furnishing the space. She could hardly believe three weeks had passed since she and Peter had moved here. The move had gone well, and she had settled in with the Weavers.

Peter seemed to be comfortable at the pastor's house, but he never made any comments one way or another about his living arrangements. She hadn't quite figured out where Peter was coming from, because they had taken little time for personal interaction. The first three weeks of work had been filled with preparations for the projects and had brought them to the middle of May. The first group of volunteers from a nearby college would arrive in a couple of days.

Ashley sank down in the chair behind her desk and stared at the monitor. She put her fingers on the keyboard, but fear froze her brain. She couldn't type. What had possessed her to think she could handle this stuff? She wasn't an organizer or someone who knew how to make sure everyone was in the right place at the right time. She was a schoolteacher, and that was all she knew.

As she took in the mountain of folders sitting on her desk, a churning sensation settled in the pit of her stomach. Was she prepared to do this job? Was this really what God wanted her to do? Why was she having doubts now? She should've dealt with them before their move, but she'd never anticipated feeling inadequate to the task.

Closing her eyes, she sank further back in the chair and prayed. *Lord, I don't know what I'm doing here. You've got to help me. I want to serve You, and if this is where You want me to serve, You have to show me the way because I can't do it on my own.*

"Are you falling asleep on the job already?"

At the sound of Peter's voice, Ashley immediately straightened in the chair. "I was just praying."

"Oh…I didn't mean to disturb you." Grimacing, he went to his desk and opened up a spreadsheet on his computer.

"No problem. I should've told you before that you might find me praying almost any time." Ashley looked at him over her shoulder. "So if you ever want to share your prayer time let me know."

He shook his head as his brow wrinkled in a little frown. "I'm one of those private prayer people. Is that okay with you?"

She shrugged. "Sure. We each have to talk to God in our own way. Personal time with God is important, but sometimes it helps to pray with other people."

"Gotcha." He turned back to the computer.

Now what should she say? Was this his way of shutting down the conversation? He was definitely immersed in the business side, and she'd been impressed with his dedication to the task of getting the project off to a good start. But she wasn't sure where he stood on the spiritual side. He went through the motions of going to church, but sometimes she doubted that his heart was in it.

She had to keep reminding herself to leave the judging to God. He was the only one who knew Peter's heart. She should tend to the dedication of her own heart to God and leave Peter's alone.

"So how are things over at the Weavers'? Jessica and Libby must keep it interesting." Peter's question caught her off guard.

"Yeah. And they love to talk." Despite her wish to have sisters, Ashley had been uncomfortable as the girls had invaded her space, wanting to talk about everything under the sun.

She'd spent too many years as a loner, even on the mission field. Though she'd lived with a missionary family, her time and space had been her own. Now she wasn't sure how to integrate her life with these lively teenagers.'

"What do they talk about?" Peter asked.

"You name it, they talk about it." Ashley released a heavy sigh. "They keep trying to give me a makeover. You know—

the clothing, makeup and hair thing? I can't imagine me as a fashion plate."

"Maybe you ought to give them speed-shopping lessons while they pick out your clothes and makeup. You could go along with it for fun."

"Maybe." Ashley started typing and hoped Peter wouldn't make any more suggestions.

His puzzling behavior had her on edge. One minute he was unwilling to talk, and the next, he was asking questions and making small talk. What had he meant about the makeover? Did he think she needed one?

Why did she care what he thought? It was dumb to care, but deep down inside, she did. Besides, he was only joking, wasn't he? But she couldn't forget he'd dated a lot of beautiful women and probably thought she was a real Plain Jane.

Over the past three weeks, he'd been charming and funny, and he'd made work fun. She'd started to like him. She'd let herself believe he wasn't that shallow, but she guessed she'd been mistaken.

A little ache pricked her heart, but she had to forget it. She had mission work to think about. She didn't need to be thinking about herself. Besides, what place would fancy clothes, hair and makeup have while they were painting and repairing houses?

Ashley glanced over the lists of names on the roster for each week. She had ensured that each person or group had a place to stay either on his or her own or with one of the local church families. Then she had to make sure she had enough workers for each project, besides planning at least two evening activities for those who wanted to participate.

Sometimes coordinating all this gave her a headache. She stopped and rubbed her temples. Teaching was much easier. She could hardly wait to get out and actually start working on the houses so she could get away from the computer.

As she scanned the list further, she came across three groups of people with the last name of Dalton. She picked up the list and walked over to Peter's desk. She held out the piece of paper and pointed to the names. "Do you know these people?"

Nodding, Peter took the paper from her and smiled. "Yeah." He tapped the paper. "These are my brothers and their families and my parents."

"They signed up to do a mission?"

"It was my mom's idea. Wait until you get to know my mother, the steamroller."

"Does she know you call her that?" Ashley asked, wondering whether Peter realized he was describing himself. Judging from his statement, he must come by his surge-ahead tactics naturally. Ashley could hardly wait to meet his family.

Peter put his head back and laughed aloud. "I don't know that I've ever said that to her face, but she knows she has a tendency to order the rest of us around."

"And does your dad stand for that?"

"My dad lets her have just enough rope so she doesn't get herself tied up in knots. I think they understand each other very well. They have a great relationship."

"So why is it that you haven't followed in their footsteps?"

He frowned. "You mean get married?"

"Yeah."

"You certainly know how to ask pointed questions."

"Yes, I'll admit that." Ashley wanted to run and hide under her desk. Why had she asked that question? It was none of her business why a man like him couldn't make a commitment even though his parents' marriage served as a good example of happiness. But curiosity got the best of her.

The phone rang. Peter looked at her and grinned. "Saved by the bell." He picked up the phone and in seconds was involved in conversation.

The phone not only saved Peter from having to answer her question, but it saved her the embarrassment of him refusing to answer. Ashley busied herself with her own work and wished she could take the question back. Add bluntness to her other problem—being fashion challenged.

After he finished talking, Peter put the receiver back in the cradle and looked her way. "That was the building supply. They're delivering the materials for our first job. I'm going over to the Browns' house to accept the shipment and make sure we have everything we ordered and also tell them where to put it. Would you like to go?"

"Are you sure that's safe? I might ask you another pointed question."

Smirking, he shook his head. "I just won't answer."

"Fair enough."

He picked up the phone again. "I'll give Ida a call and let her know we're on our way."

"Okay." Ashley closed the programs on her computer while Peter talked to Ida.

Hanging up the phone, he turned to her. "Let's take your pickup in case we need to haul something."

"Sure." Ashley grabbed her purse and headed for the door.

Her foolish heart had leapt at his invitation, only to realize it was nothing personal. He wanted to use her vehicle. She chided herself for feeling deflated. Working around him took her on an emotional roller-coaster ride, mostly of her own making.

Following him to her pickup, she tried to squash any personal feelings about Peter. But the message wasn't getting through to her heart. She promised herself not to ask any more intrusive questions. She had to learn to mind her own business. She had to remember he thought she was nosy, as well as in need of a makeover. When she started thinking of him as more than a business associate, she was asking for trouble.

Chapter Nine

As the pickup hummed along the narrow, hilly street, Peter couldn't decide whether he was finally getting used to the small town or not. There was barely a street in town that didn't either go up a hill or down one. The place often reminded him of Mayberry from the TV reruns of *The Andy Griffith Show* that he'd watched as a kid. Sometimes, he almost expected to see Opie or Sheriff Taylor moseying down the sidewalk.

During his first week in town, he'd missed the sounds of the city—honking horns, sirens and general traffic. In the last couple of days, however, he finally felt as though he was adjusting to the peacefulness, especially at night.

Ashley hadn't said a word since they'd gotten into the pickup. He was afraid he'd teased her a little too much back at the office. He was never quite sure how to talk to her. Sometimes she seemed too serious, and she was always asking those direct questions, some of which he didn't want to answer.

She had warned him that day in Helen on their first trip together that she'd be asking questions to get to know him. But mostly, she'd left him alone. She'd said they should get to know each other, but they'd been working together for three weeks now without ever getting much beyond work-related conversations. For some reason that disappointed him.

Maybe *he* should start the get-to-know-you conversation. He'd probably given her the idea that he was reluctant to talk about himself. He knew way more about her than she knew about him. He knew her favorite dish was lasagna and that she liked chocolate cake and speed shopping. She wasn't into fashion or fancy electronic gadgets. Most of all, she loved God and wanted to serve Him.

Her earlier assessment was probably right: If they were going to work closely together, they should know something about each other.

In only a few weeks, he'd learned mission work was about relationships—with people and with God. Was he going to fit in to this project? He was still constantly second-guessing himself—not familiar territory for him.

He found opening up difficult, but what was one more challenge? "I want to let you know I'm excited that we're working together. I want us to be great team."

Surprise registered on her face as she gave him a quick look and gripped the steering wheel a little tighter. "I think we can do that."

"Me, too." Now what did he say? How could he steer the conversation so they could really get to know each other without her probing into why he wasn't interested in marriage? If he started asking questions, would the discussion return to that topic? Maybe he could start with a question about the Weaver girls. "So, do you like having temporary sisters?"

Ashley didn't answer immediately. He wondered whether he'd turned the tables and put her on the spot. Was she having a difficult time finding an answer? Where was her openness now?

Finally she admitted, "I don't know."

There was an honest answer. Her candor was still intact. "What makes you say that?"

"They're still a bit overwhelming."

"But they should make the summer fun." Peter smiled as he waited for her answer.

"Time will tell."

"You don't sound too excited."

"Maybe I'll eventually get used to all the giggling exuberance." Ashley looked as though she had just tasted a lemon.

Peter tried to hold back his laughter, but he couldn't.

"You think this is funny?" Her sour expression turned to a frown.

"No, just the look on your face." He snapped his fingers. "I know what you can do."

"What?"

"Get yourself an iPod."

"Another gadget. How will that help?"

"You can tune them out."

She frowned at him again. "You're not being very nice."

"You're right. I shouldn't tease you or make fun of them. Looks like we both have our work cut out for us. I have to learn to be on my best behavior at the pastor's house, and you need to learn to live with a couple of talkative teens."

"Which one of us will have the most success?"

"Are you challenging me?"

"If that's the way you want to look at it." She stopped the pickup at the traffic light in the center of town.

Peter raised his arms and laced his fingers behind his head. "How do we determine who wins?"

"You're up for the challenge?"

"Yep."

Ashley wrinkled her freckled nose as the light turned green. "Okay, let's say whoever leaves first is the loser."

"You mean leaves the project?"

"Yes."

"Okay. You're on. We can shake on it when you're done driving." Peter lowered his arms.

"A gentlemen's agreement?"

"I wouldn't exactly call you a gentleman."

She gave him a perturbed glance. "You know what I mean."

"I guess. You know, with all the politically correct stuff going around these days, a guy doesn't always know what might offend someone. So I try to be careful."

"You can't offend me."

Peter chuckled, pretty sure that wasn't true. "I'm still not taking any chances."

"Now I know for sure you don't have sisters."

"Yeah, just brothers."

"How many, did you say?"

"Two." Peter wondered whether this could be an opening for the get-to-know-you conversation. Should he volunteer more information?

"Older or younger?"

"I'm the oldest."

"Are they single like you?"

She was bringing up the marriage thing again. He didn't want that topic to turn around to him, but maybe if he kept the topic on his brothers, he'd be okay.

"No. In fact, my middle brother, Matt, just got married a few weeks ago in South Dakota where they live. I shared best-man duties with my youngest brother, Wade."

"South Dakota?"

"Yeah, I have a cousin who lives there, too." Did he dare mention that Matt had married a well-known actress? Being out of the country for five years, Ashley might have never heard of

Rachel Carr, who had received critical acclaim for her latest movie role. Besides, maybe it would sound like bragging.

"Is Wade married?"

"Yes. Matt and I shared the best-man duties at Wade's wedding almost two years ago."

"Sounds like you're always the best man, never the groom." She gave him a sideways glance.

"And I intend to keep it that way." He smiled wryly. He might as well let her know where he stood on the subject. "Are you trying to make some kind of point?"

"No, only an observation."

Why was he worried about what Ashley thought? Marriage wasn't in the cards for him. Even though he could see how happy his brothers and his parents were in their marriages, Peter didn't have any desire to go down that path.

Oddly enough, Matt and Wade had also been the victims of broken engagements, but they'd managed to get past their broken hearts and find love again. Peter couldn't forget the hurt. He definitely wasn't pining away for his lost love, but he still wasn't interested in taking a risk on a new one.

Time to change the subject.

"So back to your challenge. What does the winner get?"

"Trying to change the subject?"

Peter chuckled. "You must read minds."

"No. Just people."

"I'll have to make a note of that."

"Adding that to your other note about including me in your future decisions for the mission project?" she asked.

So she was keeping track of what he said. She remembered his comment from three weeks ago. "I made a note of that, too? Are you making notes of my notes?"

"Someone was has to."

"And that someone is going to be you?"

"Yes."

"I can live with that." Peter laughed again. He hadn't laughed this much in a long time. She was making him laugh at himself and his tendency to make notations about everything. She was the first person who ever called attention to his penchant for mental as well as physical note-taking. *Another note to self. Beware. She remembers everything you say.* "Now who's changing the subject? Are you trying to get out of the challenge?"

"No." She shook her head. "What if we both find this is our life's work and calling and neither of us leaves?"

"You mean you've given up on your wish to go back to Africa?"

She didn't say anything. The engine's hum was the only sound in the cab. She had a white-knuckle grip on the steering wheel again. "I've finally faced the reality that I may never get to go back. If I do, then I guess you win." She let out a heavy sigh. "It makes me terribly sad that I may never return or see my friends there before we meet again in heaven."

Before we meet again in heaven. Peter let the phrase roll through his mind. When had he ever thought in such terms? His life was all about the here and now, he never thought much about heaven. That was probably why his spiritual life was pretty anemic. Ashley's perspective put him to shame.

Listening to the sadness in Ashley's voice made his heart ache. He wasn't prepared for his reaction. What was there about her that stretched his emotions? She had him laughing heartily one minute and feeling heart-wrenching sorrow the next. He looked out the passenger window as he tried to gather his thoughts. "I didn't mean to bring up something that makes you so sad."

"You didn't know."

"I should have."

"Let's not worry about it." She turned to him for a second with a fake, cheesy grin. "We'll plan not to be sad."

"You can plan not to be sad?"

"Yes, we think happy thoughts. Think about the people we're going to help this summer and the people who will be blessed because they helped do the work."

"True."

There was her Pollyanna attitude again. He had to get some of that. Would her outlook rub off on him while they worked together? It almost scared him to think about being so positive.

He had to remember she wasn't positive all of the time. She had her down moments, too. But he should let her lift him up rather than being the one to take her down. That was about as positive as he could get.

Did he dare bring up the prize for winning the challenge, or would that topic plunge them right back into those disconcerting thoughts? Unless she pursued it, he would consider the topic off-limits.

"So what do you like to do for fun?"

"Fun? That's a relative word. What's fun for one person might not be fun for the next."

"I'm not talking about just anyone. I'm talking about you."

"I love to read. Give me a book and I can go anywhere."

"But wouldn't you actually like to do something rather than read about it?"

"Sometimes. But I don't necessarily want to experience everything I read about." Ashley parked the pickup in front of Ida and Cecil's house. "Well, we're here, but I don't see a delivery truck."

"Then we'll have a few minutes to visit." Peter stepped out of the pickup and waited for Ashley to join him on the front walk.

"You know Ida will want to feed you."

Peter waggled his eyebrows. "Why do you think I came over here?"

Ashley laughed and scurried up the walk. Enjoying the sound of her laughter, he hurried to catch up. Since the day he'd picked her up at the airport, he'd been intrigued by Ashley. Now the fascination was weaving its way into his heart. Fearing that would result in hurt for both of them, he knew he should find a way to push her back out.

The smell of freshly baked cookies floated all the way to the door as Ashley stood on the Browns' front porch. She glanced at Peter as he rang the doorbell. "When did they say the truck would be here?"

Peter pulled his cell phone from his pocket and looked at it. "At two."

Ida opened the door and ushered them into the house. "I hope you brought your appetite."

Peter took a deep breath. "Do I smell cookies?"

"Chocolate chip. I made them just for you." Ida smiled up at him, her blue eyes sparkling.

"Ida, you're going to make me fat before the summer's over." He patted his trim midsection. "How's Cecil doing today?"

"A little tired. He still works with a physical therapist, and the day after the therapy he's plumb tuckered out. He's taking a nap."

"I hope all the commotion doesn't disturb him," Peter said.

Ida waved a hand at him. "You won't bother him. He's a heavy sleeper." A buzzer went off, and Ida took another sheet of cookies from the oven.

Ashley hung back and took in the exchange while Ida placed cookies on a big plate. Something about the way Peter related to the elderly woman tugged at her heart. She didn't want the scene to affect her, but it did. When Peter acted like this, the resistance she had so carefully constructed against his charm crumbled like the cookies they were about to eat.

Too many times she was finding herself thinking about him. She'd never had a serious relationship with a man. The dating she'd done in college had been with guys who were more like friends than romantic interests. She couldn't let the first guy who entered her life after she came home turn her head. Besides, she wanted a man whose main interest in life was the Lord, not money or business. Despite Peter's work with the mission project, she saw him as a money man, not a missions man.

Looking Ashley's way, Ida motioned for her to join them. "Come, come. You need some of these cookies as well. You're not one of those women who eats nothing but salads, are you?"

"No, and I love chocolate-chip cookies."

"Let's have some." Ida picked up the plate loaded with cookies. "They're still warm—I'm making them as snacks for everyone working on the house."

"They'll be a real hit. You make the best cookies." Peter grabbed a cookie off the plate and took a big bite.

Grinning widely, Ida waved a hand at him. "You're going to give me a big head if you keep braggin' on my cookies."

"I'm only being honest. If we provide you with the ingredients, would you be interested in making cookies for the workers all summer?" Peter asked.

Ida put a hand over her heart. "Oh, yes. That would give me the opportunity to do something to give back to the mission projects, but you don't have to give me the ingredients."

"Yes, we do." Ashley patted Ida on the arm. "Those expenses will go into our food budget."

Peter waved his cookie in the air. "These are so much better than store-bought cookies. So if you'll give me a list of what you need, we'll make sure you get it."

Ida hugged Peter and then Ashley. "You young people just brighten my day. Thank you."

"We should be thanking you," Ashley said.

A rumble sounded outside, and Peter went to the front door to look out. "The delivery truck's here."

While Peter went out to greet the deliverymen, Ashley

stayed in the house with Ida so she could compile the list of ingredients for her cookies. With her gnarled fingers gripping the pencil, Ida wrote her list in a shaky scrawl. After she finished, she looked up at Ashley. "Now you can give this to your handsome young man."

Taking the list from Ida, Ashley wondered whether this was a good time to correct Ida's mistaken notion that Peter and she had a relationship other than work. She couldn't continue to let Ida have the wrong impression. "Ida, Peter and I just work together. We aren't dating or anything like that."

Ida adjusted her glasses and peered at Ashley. "Then you should be. He's a fine man. I'm going to work on getting you two together. No sense in the two of you being lonely."

Ashley had no clue how to respond to Ida's plan. A funny little flutter centered in Ashley's stomach when she thought about the idea of being Peter's girlfriend. Now Ida was putting into words the feelings Ashley didn't want to acknowledge.

Peter had clearly indicated that he wasn't interested in marriage. So who was Ida or Ashley to change his mind? Not that she wanted to change his mind anyway. Maybe the best way to deal with Ida's pronouncement was to ignore it.

Ashley headed for the front door. "Let's see what they've delivered."

Ida shuffled alongside Ashley. "I knew you'd want to keep an eye on that handsome fella."

Ashley smiled, forcing herself not to comment. When they reached the front porch, Peter was giving instructions to the deliverymen. His take-charge style had the men hopping to do his bidding. Even though he was in charge, he didn't have a problem giving the other guys a hand while they unloaded. Ashley couldn't help admiring the way he got the job done. He was fair, and he commanded respect. No wonder he'd been her dad's second-in-command.

Ashley continued to watch him work. Because his business style wasn't the same as hers, she'd often cautioned herself about passing judgment on the way he did his job. She was seeing more and more each day what Peter had given up to be part of this project. How did he feel about it?

While she wondered about the answer to that question, the last of the items came off the truck. Lumber of every shape and size, cans of paint, paintbrushes, hammers, nails, saws, work-benches and a myriad of other construction needs sat on the porch or under tarps in the driveway. The truck driver handed Peter a clipboard and pen, and he signed the attached paper.

As the delivery truck drove away, Peter turned back to the house. His gaze met Ashley's, and her heart raced. She swallowed hard as she thought about everything Ida had said. Ashley couldn't let Ida's talk make her think of Peter in a romantic context, even though the idea was tempting.

Ashley put on a happy face as he approached. "Is everything in order?"

"It is. We've got the supplies we need for Monday." Peter turned his attention to Ida. "Are you ready for the big invasion?"

"I sure am. And I'll have a fresh batch of cookies for everyone."

"I can hardly wait," Peter said. "We'd better be on our way. I've got a few things to finish up at the office. See you at church on Sunday."

"Wait. I want to send some of those cookies with you. I'll be right back." Ida quickly disappeared into the house.

Peter smiled. "She's something else."

"She sure is. Asking Ida to make cookies was a wonderful gesture. You made her feel important. Thanks."

"It was nothing." Peter shrugged, seeming embarrassed.

Ida reappeared, carrying a plastic bag full of cookies. "Here you go. But don't go eating them all in one sitting."

Taking the bag, Peter laughed. "Thanks. I'll try not to. Besides, I have to share with Ashley."

"See you Sunday," Ida called as Peter and Ashley waved and headed to her pickup.

As Ashley turned the key in the ignition, she glanced at Peter. "I want to stop at the grocery store and buy the things Ida needs to make the cookies."

"More speed shopping?"

"If I need to be speedy."

He gave her a wry smile. "Take as much time as you want, but don't buy a lot because I'm sending a list of things to your dad. He'll have someone purchase everything at a discount warehouse. He'll either have someone deliver it or deliver it himself. He hasn't decided."

"When did you talk to my dad?"

"E-mail."

"Oh. Well, I'd better get Ida's stuff. Are you coming?"

Shaking his head, he held up his cell phone. "Got some calls to make."

"Okay." Ashley hurried into the grocery and tried not to be disappointed that Peter wasn't coming with her.

Chapter Ten

After they returned to the office, Ashley put the perishable grocery items in the small refrigerator, then started going over the list of families from the local church that had volunteered to keep workers during the summer. Everything was in place for the first two groups, scheduled for the last two weeks in May. Then she noticed a number of people who had no housing during the first week in June. According to the records, none was available.

She turned to Peter. "I think we have a problem with the housing in June."

"How could that be? I thought we had everyone matched with one of the church families who volunteered to provide housing." He got up from his computer and stood behind her chair.

"Yes, we did, but we had two more groups sign up."

"Didn't we put a cap on each week?"

"We did, but when these people contacted me about coming, I told them they could. They registered and sent in their money." Ashley bit her bottom lip.

He let out an exasperated sigh. "That's the reason we had the caps, so we wouldn't run into this problem. You have to have plans and stick to them."

"How can you turn away people who want to help?" She held her breath.

"Well, since you said they could come, I suggest you find them some housing." He returned to his desk and started typing.

The tone of his voice stung. Even the staccato tap of his typing sounded angry. Ashley pressed her lips together so she wouldn't come back with an ugly retort. Why was he being so hard-nosed? The people only wanted to help. They'd paid their fees for the week. So what was the problem? The problem was finding them a place to stay. *Lord, here I am again, asking for Your help. And help Peter, too.*

All of the good feelings they'd shared earlier had blown up in her face. His kindness to Ida had slipped around her defenses and made her entertain romantic thoughts again. But here he was being all business. Maybe there was no way to reconcile business practices with missions.

She wasn't used to turning people away when they wanted to help. She leaned back in the chair and rubbed her temples with her fingers. She had two weeks to work on getting housing for these people. How was she going to do it?

After Ashley left the office, she wanted to go back to her room, close the door and lick her wounds. But as soon as she walked into the Weavers' house, Jessica and Libby descended on her like two vultures over roadkill. Ashley definitely felt like roadkill after her confrontation with Peter.

Less than half an hour after their disagreement, Peter had left the office with barely a goodbye. Her heart was heavy. She hated leaving disputes unresolved. She wanted time to herself to try to think through the mess. The last thing she wanted to do was spend time with Jessica and Libby.

"Hey, Ashley, Mom's taking us shopping at the Mall of Georgia and the outlet mall near Dawsonville tomorrow. We want you to go with us. Okay?" Libby looked at Ashley with expectation written all over her face.

"Tomorrow?"

"Yeah. We're planning to spend the whole day," Jessica said. "Please say you'll go."

Shopping. Was this a test from God? Surviving a day of shopping should be easy. Maybe she could find a nice little gift for Ida and Cecil. "Okay."

Both of the teens erupted into a cheer, and they hugged Ashley. "We'll tell Mom," Jessica called over her shoulder as they raced off toward the kitchen.

Ashley saw this as her chance to escape to her room. Maybe if she closed the door, she might get some privacy. Was that too much to ask? She took the stairs two at a time and hurried into her room. She closed the door, kicked off her shoes and flung herself onto the bed. Lacing her fingers behind her head, she stared at the ceiling.

She should pray, but she didn't feel like praying. Her heart was too full of disappointment. She shouldn't let Peter's attitude get to her, but it did. She should read her Bible, but she couldn't concentrate. Her mind buzzed with the day's events.

Finally, she picked up the Bible with its tattered leather binding and let it fall open. She looked at the page staring back at her. An underlined passage in the Gospel of Matthew jumped out at her: "But I tell you: Love your enemies and pray for those who persecute you."

Peter wasn't her enemy. He wasn't persecuting her, although his attitude almost made it feel that way. What he said to her was probably right. She had to learn to go by the plans. If she didn't, they'd be in a mess every week. Nothing would go right. Plans were made to be followed. Following God's plan was the most important thing. She needed to put aside her hurt feelings and find a way to work with Peter. She should pray.

Before she started her prayer, a knock sounded on the door. Probably Jessica and Libby again with more of their plans. Ashley wanted to tell them to go away, but she didn't need to alienate more people. "Come in."

The door swung open. Jessica and Libby stood in the hallway. Giggling, Jessica stepped into the room. "We're going to put highlights in our hair. You wanna do it, too?"

Ashley's first thought was *no*. She glanced at Jessica, who held the box containing a highlighting kit. "Does your mother know you're doing this?"

Nodding, Libby pranced into the room. "She said we could, but she doesn't want to hear about it if we don't like it."

"I don't think highlights are my thing." Ashley got off the bed. "You girls can do it but not me. I'll help you, if you want."

"Yes, we want your help, but…like…you have to do it, too." Jessica shoved the box at her. "Here. Read the directions."

Ashley took the box and studied the instructions. "I'm not sure I can do this right."

"Sure you can. It'll be fun." Libby danced around the room. "One of our friends did it. She said it was easy."

"After we get done, we'll help you do yours." Jessica lifted a strand of Ashley's hair off her shoulder. "Your hair will look really good with highlights."

Shrinking back, Ashley raised her eyebrows. "This might be okay for y'all, but I don't think—"

"Yes, you should. Peter will notice."

Ashley frowned. "What does Peter have to do with it?"

"You kind of like him, don't you?"

"Of course, I like him." Why would they think she had some interest in Peter other than their working relationship? Were they seeing something she didn't want to admit? Her stomach sank. Had Peter noticed, too?

"We don't mean just *like* him. We mean you're attracted to him. And he's attracted to you."

Ashley raised her eyebrows again. "He is?"

"Yeah, he's always hovering around you, looking at you when you don't notice. And you do the same thing to him. He always sits with you in church." Libby looked at Ashley as if she was daring her to deny the assessment.

"His sitting with me in church doesn't mean a thing."

Jessica shrugged and smiled mischievously. "Maybe, maybe not."

Ashley sank down on the bed. Could it possibly be? No. He only noticed women who looked like fashion models.

"Girls, Peter's a very handsome man, but he only dates people who look like they should be on the cover of a fashion magazine. You're misinterpreting his actions. We work together, and he knows me better than anyone else here. Of course he's going to sit with me."

Libby smiled and joined Ashley on the bed. "You're pretty, too, Ashley. You have beautiful hair, and the highlights will make it stand out. Wait and see."

A helpless feeling overcame Ashley as she looked from one teenage girl to the other. First Ida, and now Jessica and Libby were trying to push her and Peter together. How had it happened that two teenagers were trying to play matchmakers? And why was she going to let them?

Because she was finally admitting to herself that she wanted Peter's attention.

As Peter entered the church Sunday morning, he walked down the aisle toward the front amid introductions and handshakes. Everyone here was so friendly. He couldn't help thinking of the old country church where his brother Matt had recently gotten married. The people there were friendly, too.

Despite the similarities between the two churches with their congenial congregations and nearly identical dark pews and woodwork, the worship services were quite dissimilar.

Even after attending church here for several Sundays, Peter wasn't used to the guitars and drums that were part of the service. The church he attended in Atlanta had what they called a contemporary service, but he'd always chosen to go to the more formal, traditional service, the same one his parents and Richard attended. Ashley seemed to enjoy the contemporary style of worship as she sang the words to the lively tunes that were unfamiliar to him. Every Sunday she smiled up at him while he stood there feeling out of place.

He searched for Ashley and finally spotted her in the third pew from the front. Her honey-colored hair seemed to sparkle in the overhead lights. His heart twisted when he realized she had her head bowed and appeared to be praying. Maybe he should pray—pray for forgiveness. He'd treated her badly the other day, and he hoped he could make amends today. He feared she might not speak to him, but that wasn't in her nature.

He had to do more than pray for forgiveness. He had to ask her to forgive him. It seemed as though he'd done more praying in the past three weeks than he'd done in his entire life. Was she praying for him? He probably didn't deserve her prayers. More than likely she was praying for the people she'd left in Africa or for the upcoming workdays. He wondered if he could ever begin to have the kind of spiritual life that she had.

As the songs began, Peter slipped into the pew beside Ashley. She glanced at him with a surprised smile tugging at the corners of her mouth—a very kissable mouth. As the idea zinged through his brain, he nearly dropped his Bible. She smiled. That was good, but his sudden notion about kissing her was not. Maybe she could forgive him, but not if he acted on that crazy impulse.

Somehow she looked different. He tried to figure out what had changed. With her sweet soprano voice gracing the song, she clapped along with the lively tune. He remembered Ashley's mentioning how the folks in Africa sang such wonderful praises to God. What was their service like? Was she still missing the people she cared about so much?

When Pastor Cummings started his sermon, Peter's mind whirled with thoughts of how he was going to apologize to Ashley. Saying he was sorry was difficult for him, and admitting he was wrong didn't come easily. He prided himself in doing the right thing at the right time so he wouldn't have to say he was sorry for anything. But this time maybe the words were necessary.

The service ended, but before Peter could speak to Ashley, Ida and Cecil captured her attention. Then Jessica and Libby cornered her. At this rate, he'd never get to apologize.

Then a tall, balding man walked up to him. "Hi, I'm Lawrence Moore. You're Peter Dalton, the guy in charge of the mission projects, right?"

"Yes. What can I do for you?"

"I wanted to make sure I have the right information. Are we supposed to pick up the people who are staying with us this evening?"

"Yes. Plan to meet in the church parking lot around seven tonight. Thanks for volunteering."

"You're welcome. We're looking forward to it. It'll be fun to have some young people around our house again."

Peter saw this as his chance to intercept Ashley before she got away. "Lawrence, wait right here, and I'll introduce you to the person who'll be matching people with their guests tonight."

"Okay."

Peter hurried after Ashley, who was walking down one of the side aisles to the door. He touched her lightly on one arm.

She turned, and his heart jumped into his throat when their eyes met. "I've got someone who'd like to meet you."

"You do?" Surprise registered in her eyes. "Who wants to meet me?"

"One of the folks who's providing housing for the week."

"Oh, good."

"Follow me." Peter breathed a sigh of relief as she followed him back toward the front of the building.

Peter made the introductions. Then he listened while Ashley and Lawrence discussed the week ahead. In minutes, she had the man and his wife not only taking people into their home, but also volunteering to work on Ida and Cecil's house. Peter realized Ashley had a gift when it came to dealing with people. He'd been completely wrong to chastise her for allowing more folks to work on the project. He could hardly wait to make amends.

He was starting to ask Ashley to go to lunch with him when Jessica called to Ashley from the back of the sanctuary. Peter turned to see Jessica and Libby coming up the aisle.

Jessica rushed up to Ashley. "Mom and Dad said to meet them at the restaurant."

Libby joined them and looked at Peter. "Peter, you can come, too, if you want."

"Thanks. I will." Glad for the invitation, Peter followed the trio as they left the church.

When they reached the parking lot, Jessica turned and looked at Peter, then waved a hand at Ashley. "Doesn't Ashley look great in her new outfit? We went shopping yesterday, and we all got new stuff. And we put highlights in our hair."

Peter looked Ashley over from head to toe. Her brown and white floral top had a little belt that tied around her slim waist. The top matched the ruffled brown skirt that stopped just above her knees. Now he realized why she looked different.

She looked terrific. Maybe he would've realized before if he hadn't been trying to concentrate on the sermon rather than on the thought of kissing her.

Did he dare tell Ashley she looked great, or would she bristle at the compliment? On the other hand, if he didn't say she looked nice, what would she think? How did a guy handle these questions? He never used to have this much trouble knowing what to say to women. What had happened to him?

"Yeah, she looks very nice. You all do. And I like the hair." His compliment was lame, but he didn't want to embarrass himself or Ashley by saying too much.

"Thanks." A pink tinge was already creeping up Ashley's cheeks while she wrinkled her freckled nose.

Her cute little nose. Oh, man. She was turning his brain to mush. How stupid that he hadn't figured out why Ashley looked different today. She'd actually let the Weaver girls give her a little fashion advice.

He hurried to his SUV. If only he had some reason to ride with Ashley rather than driving his own vehicle to the restaurant. But he wouldn't be alone with her because Jessica and Libby would be there, too. So he couldn't talk with her anyway. With a couple of afternoon meetings and a church softball game, he didn't see any opportunities for time alone with Ashley today.

When would he get a chance to make his apologies for Friday's blunder?

When Peter arrived at the ball field later that afternoon, the softball game was well underway. As he took a seat on the bleachers, he noticed a dark-haired boy standing off to the side while all of the adults and kids played ball. Peter watched for a while, then finally approached him. "Hi, what's your name?"

The boy looked up at him, his brown eyes startled. "Tim."

Peter held out his hand. "I'm Peter. Do you want to play ball?"

The youngster shook Peter's hand. "Maybe, but no one picked me to play on their team."

"We'll have to do something about that." Peter studied the scrawny, bespectacled little kid. He understood what it meant not to be picked. He could laugh about it now, but he'd once been that kid who hadn't been very good at playing ball. There was nothing funny about being the kid that the others didn't want on their team.

Shrugging, Tim shook his head. "I'm not sure I'm good enough."

"Everyone's good enough for this game." Peter wondered why anyone, especially Ashley, would allow the little boy to sit out by himself while everyone else played. She wasn't the type of person to ignore a lonely child.

Peter scanned the ball field. His heart took a little leap when he spied Ashley standing in right field. She'd pulled her hair into a ponytail and stuck it through the opening in the back of her ball cap. She looked almost like a little kid in her T-shirt, jeans, sneakers and a glove that looked way too big for her. Jessica and Libby had coerced Ashley into coming to the game, but he never guessed she'd actually play.

When the team up to bat made their last out, Peter looked at Tim. "Wait here while I see if you can get in the game."

Peter trotted toward Ashley who was coming in from the outfield. While they'd eaten lunch today with the Weavers, she had treated him as if he'd never said a harsh word to her. Her kind treatment made him feel even worse, and still, he didn't see a chance to apologize. He waved to her.

Smiling, she came his way. "Hi, I see you finally arrived."

"Yeah. The meeting took longer than I thought it would, but now everything's set for next week." Peter glanced back at Tim, who still sat on the bleachers. "You got a place for another player?"

"You want to play?"

"No. Tim does." Peter motioned toward the boy, sitting on the other end of the bleachers.

Ashley glanced in that direction. "Tim? He said he didn't want to play when we started. He said he only wanted to watch."

"He changed his mind."

"Okay. We'll find him a spot on one of the teams."

Peter leaned closer and whispered, "He says he's not very good. I want to help him out a little. Maybe that was why he said he didn't want to play. I could practice with him and give him some confidence before he goes out on the field."

"Good idea." Ashley motioned toward the backstop. "There are a few bats and balls in that bag. You could practice with him before I put him in the game. What do you think?"

"Great idea. Thanks."

"This is really nice of you to help him out. He doesn't seem to know how to fit in."

Peter nodded. "I kind of gathered that from the way he was hanging back."

Within minutes Peter and Tim were throwing a softball back and forth behind the backstop. Then Peter took him out to the parking lot and threw a few pitches to give him a little batting practice. Tim did surprisingly well. Peter smiled to himself. He'd never pictured himself working with kids.

Finally Ashley's team was ready to take the field again. She called to Peter and motioned him to bring Tim over to talk to her.

"Hi, Tim," Ashley said.

"Hi." The little boy's voice was barely above a whisper.

"Are you ready to get in the game now?"

Looking down, he shrugged. "I guess."

"You can take my place in right field." She handed him her glove.

"Thanks." His face brightened as he pounded one fist into the glove. "This works great."

As the youngster trotted out to right field, Peter glanced at Ashley. "I didn't mean you had to give up your spot on the team."

Ashley laughed. "I'm not giving up anything. I was only out there because they needed another player. Believe me. When Jessica and Libby insisted I come, I had only planned to watch."

"Mind if I watch with you?" Peter asked.

"Unless you want to play, too."

Smiling, Peter headed to the bleachers where a handful of spectators was cheering on the teams. "I didn't come dressed to play ball."

She looked him over. "Yeah, I'd say you might have a little trouble running the bases in a pair of loafers."

"Wonder what the story is with Tim."

Ashley shook her head. "I'm not sure. He came with the Bartons, one of the church families. Mrs. Barton told me Tim often plays with her boys. But he sure didn't want to get in the game when we started."

Suddenly, there was a crack of a bat and the ball sailed into right field. Peter held his breath as Tim stuck his gloved hand into the air. When the ball landed in the glove, Peter breathed a sigh of relief and applauded Tim's catch.

"I'm so glad he caught it," Ashley said.

"You and me both." Peter remembered the embarrassment of dropping a ball and receiving the ridicule of his fellow teammates. The ridicule had made him more determined to succeed. Eventually, he had a growth spurt and developed better coordination. Then he worked hard to prove everyone wrong when they said he'd never be an athlete. He'd definitely been a late bloomer.

But as Peter sat beside Ashley, he realized he'd dropped the ball with her. When was he going to get the opportunity to have that private conversation to make things right?

Chapter Eleven

The following day, the bad business with Ashley still ate at Peter until he could think of nothing else. His intense working style had clashed with her *laissez-faire* attitude. His instant assessment of the situation had led to his irritation, and he'd taken it out on her. Now Monday was nearly over, and he feared he still wouldn't find a time to talk with Ashley alone so he could apologize.

The sounds of hammers and saws filled the warm spring air as he checked out the progress on the Browns' porch. Most of the old floorboards had been removed, and the college kids were hard at work nailing down the new ones. Some of the local church folks were scraping the old paint from the siding. The progress so far astounded Peter. He had never thought volunteers could do such good work.

He'd spent most of the day supervising the outdoor work while Ashley had been inside doing the prep work involved with painting the interior. Not once did time for a private conversation present itself.

As Peter entered the house, a CD player sitting in the living room played contemporary Christian music. He had hoped to find Ashley alone, but two college girls were working with her. They were on their hands and knees as they put masking tape along the baseboards.

His heart took a little leap when she looked his way. Her honey-colored hair, now full of platinum-blonde highlights, was pulled back in a ponytail much as it had been yesterday while she played ball. She'd traded in her new clothes for a pair of well-worn jeans and a T-shirt that read, "Jesus loves you."

He stepped closer. "How's it going in here?"

She smiled. "Great. We're almost done with the prep work in the rooms downstairs. We'll probably start painting tomorrow."

"Good. Do you have a minute?"

She glanced at her watch, then immediately stood. "I'm sorry, no. I had no idea it was this late. I've got to get back to the Weavers'. I told Teresa I'd help with the dinner preparations. You know they're having a cookout in their backyard tonight for the workers, right?"

"Yeah." Peter sighed.

"I've got to go right now." Ashley handed Peter a roll of masking tape. "Maybe you can help them finish."

"Okay." He barely got the word out before she grabbed her purse and left the room. If he didn't know better, he'd think she was actually trying to avoid him. He glanced at the two girls. "Do you need help?"

"No, we're almost finished," one girl said.

"Okay, I'll check on the rest of the crews." Peter strode through the house to the kitchen. One of Ida's cookies might be in order to ease his disappointment in not getting to talk with Ashley. One way or another he was going to make sure he finally got to talk to her tonight.

The smell of grilling hot dogs and hamburgers filled the air. Ashley put a huge bowl of potato salad next to the pot full of baked beans. A mountain of hot dog and hamburger buns sat at one end of the table, and coolers full of lemonade and iced tea sat at the other end. Teresa Weaver set plastic plates and utensils next to the buns. Ida placed a plate of her now-famous chocolate-chip cookies on the table.

Ashley smiled at Ida, who'd insisted she should help serve the food. "Your cookies have been a hit all day."

"Thank you. I'm so excited to help. And our house…oh, my, it's going to look wonderful." Ida clapped her hands together, then hugged Ashley. "That Peter of yours is a good organizer."

"Yes, he's got everything under control." Ashley had given up trying to convince Ida that Peter wasn't hers.

Ashley was having a hard time not thinking about Peter in the same way. Such thinking was asking for trouble, but she couldn't forget how he'd looked at her in church on Sunday or how he'd helped Tim. Still, she had to remember how angry he'd been on Friday. She'd been on an emotional roller-coaster ride for days. Now he wanted to talk to her.

Ida patted Ashley on the back. "Why don't you run along and sit with him? Teresa and I have the food under control."

Ashley searched the yard where people sat at picnic tables or stood around talking in little groups. She didn't see Peter anywhere. Finally, she spotted him passing a football across the yard to one of the young men. Tim was right beside Peter, with hero worship written all over his face.

She couldn't bother Peter because he was busy, so she found Jessica and Libby and plopped down next to them at a nearby picnic table. "How was school today?"

"Lame." Jessica pouted. "Mom wouldn't let us skip school to help. She wouldn't even let us come over after school because she said we had to study."

"School's important. Final exams are coming up, aren't they?" Ashley asked.

"Yeah. You sound like Mom," Libby said.

"Well, she's right. Besides, you're getting to hang out with everyone tonight." Ashley gestured around the yard.

Jessica leaned closer to Ashley. "Yeah, but we didn't really get to meet anyone. See that guy over there passing the football to Peter? He's cool."

Ashley looked at him. She could see why the young man with his tall, muscled frame would catch the teenaged girl's eye. Ashley turned back to Jessica and laughed. "So you really aren't concerned about helping. You just want to meet the guys?"

Jessica gave Ashley an annoyed look. "No, we wanted to help, but it doesn't hurt to have good-looking guys around, too."

"Maybe Peter will introduce you," Ashley said.

"Do you think?"

Ashley nodded. "We're going to have a devotion time tomorrow night. Your mom will probably let you go to that, won't she?"

"Will you talk to her about it?"

"Sure. Do you girls plan to help after school's out for the summer?"

Libby nodded. "We both have part-time jobs, so we'll have to work around those."

"We'll fit you in whenever you can work."

A sharp whistle sounded across the yard. Ashley turned toward the sound. Pastor Rob stood near the table laden with food. He waved his hand in the air as people ceased their activities and gravitated toward him. "The ladies tell me the food is ready, so let's have a prayer."

The yard grew quiet, and everyone bowed their heads for the prayer. A dog barked in the distance as the pastor gave thanks for the food. Ashley gave silent thanks for this new chance to serve and also prayed that she would know how to deal with Peter and their differences.

After the prayer, everyone lined up to get food. Conversation and laughter filled the air as folks proceeded through the line. Buddy Weaver joked with folks as he served hot dogs and hamburgers from the grill.

Ashley found a seat at one of the picnic tables along with Jessica and Libby and the two college girls, Sarah and Nicole, who'd helped with the prep work. "So, are you exhausted after your first day?"

"I'm not tired, but my knees are sore from kneeling. We sure could use some kneepads." Laughing, Sarah pushed her dark-brown hair behind one ear.

"Yeah," Nicole said. "My mom has a kneeling pad she uses when she works in the yard. I wish I had it."

"I'll see if I can get some at one of the stores in town," Ashley said.

Peter, Tim and two of the college guys approached the table. One of them was the young man who'd drawn Jessica's attention. Peter looked at Ashley, then glanced around the table. "We can sit here, guys."

Jessica's face brightened with a smile as she scooted over. "Sure. There's room right here."

The guys found seats. Peter sat across the table from Ashley, leaving the younger kids at the other end. Peter introduced Drew and Brandon to Jessica and Libby. Jessica immediately began to quiz Drew about college life. Soon, the four college students were selling Jessica and Libby on the advantages of attending their small Christian college.

Peter joined in the conversation, joking and laughing with the group. Sitting by quietly, Ashley took in the conversation with a bit of amusement, knowing that Jessica's main interest centered on guys. How different her teenage years had been. Guys had been completely off her radar when she was in high school. Now there was only one guy in her sight—Peter.

She looked up. He was looking at her. Her heart fluttered. Feeling self-conscious, she took a big bite of her hot dog and chewed slowly.

"Good hot dog?" Peter asked, still looking at her.

Nodding, she finished the bite she'd taken. "Nothing like a grilled hot dog slathered with mustard."

"Looks like you're slathered with mustard, too." With a napkin in one hand, he reached across the table and wiped her cheek.

Taken off guard, Ashley grabbed for her own napkin and wiped madly at her face. "Why didn't you tell me I had mustard on my face?"

Winking at her, he laughed. "I just did. You look good in yellow."

"Thank you, I guess."

"I think she looks good in mustard, too." Tim laughed along with Peter.

Ashley gave Tim a poke in the ribs. "Okay, little man, are you taking lessons from Mr. Peter?"

"Yeah. He's a good teacher." Tim sat up straighter. "Did you see me catch the ball in the game?"

"I sure did, and you're right. Mr. Peter's a very good teacher."

"Thanks." Surprise written in his eyes, Peter smiled at her. Then one of the college guys asked him a question and drew his attention away from her.

She didn't know how to take his teasing or his jovial manner tonight. She wasn't sure what to make of him. Today, he wasn't the same angry man she'd dealt with on Friday. He wasn't even the same serious guy who'd attended church on Sunday or the construction supervisor who'd put together a plan for the Browns' house.

As they continued to eat, a big, burly man with dark hair sauntered toward their table. When Tim saw him, he jumped up and ran to greet him. "Dad, you got home."

"Hey, son. I said I'd make it home tonight." The man ruffled Tim's hair.

Tim grabbed his dad's hand and dragged him over to the table. "Mr. Peter, I want you to meet my dad."

Peter stood and shook hands. "Hi, I'm Peter Dalton."

"Rex Kelly. I want to thank you for helping Tim the other day. He told me about the ball game while I was on the road."

"It was my pleasure. You have a great son."

Taking in the conversation, Ashley recognized one more of Peter's good qualities. He helped people. He'd even helped her get more organized.

As soon as the guys finished eating, they started playing touch football. Since Tim was too young to play, he cheered from the sidelines. Taking charge of one of the teams, Peter stepped into the captain's role with ease.

All of the different sides of his personality paraded through her mind as she watched. He could laugh at himself, share his talents, help others and keep things in order. On one too many occasions she'd probably misjudged him. Was that the result of her own insecurity?

Ashley was finally admitting to herself why she looked at Peter so harshly. He was slowly worming his way into her heart, and that scared her. From the beginning she'd been attracted to his good looks and charm, but now his kindness and the way he related to the kids made her care about him in a whole new way.

That was why his suggestion about going along with the makeover had hurt so much when he'd first mentioned it. She wanted him to like her for herself, not because she was Richard Hiatt's daughter or because she looked good when she wore the right clothes and makeup. She wanted him to like her—Ashley Hiatt. Plain old Ashley Hiatt. Why had she let herself care about this man?

* * *

Night settled over the landscape as Peter dumped the last of the trash bags in the bins at the side of the Weavers' garage. Everything about the day had gone well, except he'd never had a chance to talk to Ashley alone. Helping to clean, he hoped, would finally give him the opportunity to make his apology for the way he'd chastised her on Friday.

So much time had passed since then. He was tempted not to bring it up, but the apology had to be made. If he let it go, the guilt would eat at him every time he looked at her. As he walked back to the house, he gazed up at the stars twinkling in the ink-black sky.

"You don't see stars like this in Atlanta, do you?" Ashley's voice came out of the darkness.

Peter looked toward the porch. She stood silhouetted against the light coming through the windows. His heart skipped a beat. "No, you don't."

"That's one of the nice things about being away from the city." She came down the steps onto the walk.

Moving toward her, he wondered whether she was thinking of the countryside in Africa. He would ask, but he was afraid to bring it up for fear it would make her sad. He hated to think of her being unhappy, especially when he was the cause. Maybe this would be his chance to apologize. "Do you have a minute?"

Even in the dim light, he recognized the concern in her expression. "I was just headed to the store."

Peter chuckled. "For a woman who claims she doesn't like to shop, you sure do a lot of it."

"I'm shopping for other people."

"For whom are you shopping now?"

"For the mission project. I'm going to look for kneepads to use while we put masking tape on the baseboards."

"Is this going on the mission credit card?"

"Only if you say so, Mr. Money Man." She bowed to him.

For a moment, he felt as though she'd punched him in the gut. Did she think he only cared about the money? "I was only joking, Ashley."

"Oh." She shrugged. "Well, I have to go shopping, so I guess we can't talk now."

He fell into step beside her as she went to her pickup. Was she trying to get away? Trying to avoid him? He couldn't let that happen. "Do you mind if I go with you?"

Looking up at him, she narrowed her gaze. "You must like to shop as much as I do."

He let out a loud guffaw. "Maybe so. I did some shopping on Saturday. I went to the closest discount warehouse on the north side of Atlanta and bought most of our supplies for the summer."

"Where'd you put them?"

"Some at the office and some at the church."

"Is there some reason you went without me?" She stopped before she stepped off the curb in front of her pickup.

"I didn't know you were expecting to go along."

"We're working together on this project, aren't we?"

"Yeah, but I was at loose ends on Saturday and figured it was a good use of my time." Peter couldn't believe he'd done the wrong thing again. He'd made a decision without consulting her. He'd never considered taking her—he'd wanted time alone to sort out his feelings after he'd jumped all over her.

"You could've at least mentioned it."

"Okay. I probably should've asked you, but then you'd have missed shopping with Jessica and Libby."

She pressed her lips together in a grim line. "You think it was a party? You should have to go shopping with them. I've never been in and out of so many dressing rooms in my life. I was beginning to feel like a mannequin. They kept finding more and more things for me to try on."

Peter couldn't help laughing. "Yeah, but you came away with some new clothes."

"So you approve of their choices? You approve of their attempt to make me over? You thought it was such a good idea." Her voice raised a notch with each sentence.

Did he dare answer those questions? No matter what he said, it wasn't going to be right. How had he gotten himself into this mess? All he wanted to do was apologize, but he'd made things worse. He gazed up into the starry night. If aliens in spaceships zoomed by right now, he'd gladly hitch a ride.

Why was he thinking of aliens? He should be thinking about God. A little prayer was in order. He sent a silent petition heavenward. *Lord, I realize I need to rely on You more. Please help me make things right with Ashley.*

When he looked back at her, she was staring at him with concern. "Are you all right?"

"Yeah. Why?"

"You had the strangest look on your face. Are my new clothes that bad?"

Shaking his head, Peter smiled. "What do you think of your new clothes? Do *you* like them?"

"I asked you first."

Peter held up his hands as if he were being robbed. "I know you did. But I'm going to be perfectly honest here—"

"You don't like them," she blurted before he could finish his sentence.

"I didn't say that. When you asked me the question, I had no idea whether you liked or disliked the new clothes. If I said I liked them and you didn't, then I'd upset you. If I said I didn't like them and you did, then I'd still upset you. I couldn't win."

Ashley leaned back against the hood of the pickup and looked at him. "I didn't mean to make it so difficult."

"I'm sure you didn't." He had the strange urge to pull her

into his embrace and just hold her. He opened the passenger side door in order to keep himself from doing that very thing—something that would probably get him into more trouble than he was already in. "If you plan to shop, we'd better get going, or the store will be closed before we get there."

"You're right." She hurried around the front of the pickup and jumped inside.

At least he was finally right about something.

"By the way, I honestly like your new clothes." He didn't miss the little smile that she tried to hide as she buckled her seatbelt. Maybe he'd still find a way to make his apology.

When they arrived at the store, Ashley hopped out and looked back at him when he didn't join her. "Aren't you coming?"

"I'll wait here."

"Then why did you come?"

Because I wanted to be with you. The words popped into his brain, but he managed not to say them. Thinking them was bad enough. "I needed to talk to you, and this seemed like a good time to do it."

"Talk to me about what?"

He motioned for her to go. "Do your shopping. When you get back, I'll explain."

"Okay. It better be good if I have to wait to hear it."

Oh, yeah. He'd better come up with something good. As she hurried across the parking lot and into the store, Peter prayed again for God to help him. Ashley had no idea how she was helping his prayer life. He'd love to watch her race through the aisles, but he needed to stay here and formulate his apology. He couldn't seem to think straight when she was around.

Peter barely had time to get his thoughts together before Ashley came out of the store. His pulse raced in time with her rapid footsteps. He took a deep breath as she got into the pickup. She held up her bag. "Mission accomplished. Kneepads.

Thankfully, you can find just about anything in that place." Turning, she put the bag in the backseat, then looked at him. "Okay, what did you want to tell me?"

He stared back at her in the dim glow coming from the parking lot lights. Why was he, a man who'd presented detailed construction plans to corporate boards, suddenly tongue-tied? He wanted this to come out right, but every time he tried to talk to Ashley recently, he didn't make sense, even to himself.

"Well, I'm listening."

"Good." *Yes. Good.* He'd finally managed to say something. He took another deep breath.

"Are you trying to give me some bad news?" Her eyebrows knit in a little frown.

"No. No. Um… Let's go back to the Weavers'. I need to show you something I left in my car." Now not only was he losing his ability to speak coherently, but he was losing his memory, too. He'd left the little gift he'd bought for Ashley in his SUV.

"Okay, if that's what you want." She drove back to the Weavers' house without making another comment.

After she parked, he jumped out of the pickup and sprinted to his SUV. He grabbed the little blue-and-white flowered gift bag from the front seat. Closing the door, he searched for Ashley. She stood on the walk.

He swallowed a lump in his throat as he approached her. Holding out the bag, he saw her surprised expression, even in the dim light. "Here's a little something for you."

"Why are you giving me another gift?" Taking the bag, she gazed at him with skepticism.

Peter released a long, slow breath. He hoped he could explain the gift. "When I went shopping for supplies, I saw this and thought of you. I wanted to make up for the way I spoke to you on Friday. I hope you'll accept it as a peace offering."

Chapter Twelve

Not daring to speculate about what lay nestled in the blue and white polka-dotted tissue paper, Ashley slowly pushed it aside and peeked inside. She spotted a small rectangular box wrapped in more of the same paper. Her heart racing, she pulled it out of the bag and held it in one hand, the bag in the other.

She hoped whatever was in the box was something she would be able to accept graciously. She ripped into the tissue paper and exposed a clear plastic container. Looking more closely she read the label. An iPod shuffle.

She glanced up at him. He stood absolutely still and seemed to be holding his breath. She could tell by the look in his eyes that he wanted her to like it. His expression made her heart twist. "You said I should get one of these things. Thank you."

"You're welcome. Now you can listen to it instead of Jessica and Libby's chatter."

Ashley couldn't help laughing. "That's true, but I'm getting used to the chatter. You really didn't have to get me anything. The mess with the housing *was* my fault."

"Yeah, but I shouldn't have gotten angry. Am I forgiven?"

Ashley took in Peter's contrite expression. He hadn't exactly said he was sorry, but she supposed the gift was close enough. "Yes. Am I?"

"Of course. Do you know how to use one of these?"

She laughed. "What do you think?"

"Okay. Dumb question. I'll show you."

"Sure, but let's sit on the porch." Ashley headed up the walk and tried not to read anything into this gift. He was making an apology the best way he knew how. It was his way of saying "I'm sorry" without having to actually say the words. She gave herself a mental shake as she sat in a wooden rocker. Peter was giving her a gift, and she still had a blip of negativity cross her mind. *Lord, forgive me.*

He picked up a nearby chair and set it beside hers. "It's charged and ready to use, and I've already downloaded a bunch of those contemporary Christian songs you like."

"When did you do this?"

"Saturday night after I finished unloading the supplies." He leaned closer. "I wasn't sure which songs you like best, but it's easy to change them."

"How many songs are on here?"

"I didn't count, but quite a few."

She opened the plastic case and removed the shuffle. Holding it in her hand, she looked over at Peter.

"Here." He reached for it. "I'll show you how it works."

"Okay."

Their fingers brushed as he took it from her. His touch made her heart race. She wasn't surprised, he was beginning to grow on her in so many ways, and not just because he'd given her another gift. Did she dare let herself care about this man in a way that meant more than their working relationship or friendship? Maybe she was developing a hopeless crush on an unattainable man, but she wasn't going to fight it.

He began to explain how the iPod worked, as he showed her the earphones, the cord for charging it and how to turn it on and off. She wasn't sure she was going to remember any of it, with him leaning so close, she had a hard time concentrating. She was sure she'd have to ask for another demonstration, but that wouldn't be so bad.

"Okay. You try it." He took her hand and placed the shuffle in her open palm.

While he held her hand, she almost forgot to breathe. Finally, she took the iPod and tried to remember what he'd told her. If she couldn't operate the thing, either he'd think she was really slow to catch on or hadn't been paying attention. She put the earphones in her ears and turned it on.

Glancing up at him, she frowned. "I don't hear anything."

"You forgot to press the center." He reached over and touched it.

A contemporary version of "Amazing Grace" sounded in her ears. She smiled at him. "Thank you. This is wonderful."

"Glad you like it." He stood. "Better call it a night. Have to go into the office before I go to Ida and Cecil's tomorrow."

"Do I need to go into the office?"

"If you don't have any work, there's no need."

Shutting off the music, Ashley shrugged. "I hate to admit this, but sometimes I don't know whether I have work to do. I'm not a businessperson. I know about missions. I know about teaching school. That's all."

Peter resumed sitting. "You know about loving God and loving people. Isn't that enough? Besides, this is about missions, not business."

"But I'm realizing there's a business side to all this. You've taught me that."

"Then we've taught each other. We're actually becoming a team." He stood again and moved toward the front steps.

Ashley followed. "Oh, I forgot to tell you I took care of the housing problem."

"You did?" He turned to look back at her.

"You didn't think I could?"

"No. I'm just surprised you were able to do it so quickly."

"I have connections."

"Who?"

"Daddy?"

"What does he have to do with the housing?"

"He bought that house we stayed in a few weeks ago. He's closing on it before the end of the month, and he said we could use it however we needed."

Peter shook his head. "That was fast. So how are you going to use it?"

"We have a couple of youth groups booked for those two weeks, and we can have them and their chaperones camped out in the house."

"You do nice work."

"Yeah, after I get called on the carpet."

Peter laughed halfheartedly. "Don't let a bear of a coworker get you down."

"That's okay. When he comes to his senses, he buys me gifts to make up for it."

Chuckling, Peter shook his head. "Have I started a trend? Does this mean every time I mess up, I have to buy you something?"

"No. I never expected you to buy me gifts."

"I know, but sometimes the giver gets more out of it than the receiver."

"You mean like 'It's better to give than receive'?"

"Yeah, something like that. A good way to salve my conscience." He turned to go again. "I have to get going."

"Good night."

"I'll see you tomorrow."

"Okay." Ashley waved as Peter jogged to his SUV.

A tender place for him settled in her heart. Something had changed between them tonight. They'd gone beyond friendship. She looked at the shuffle and what it represented—Peter's way of making things right between them. Could this lead to something more? She couldn't believe she was even thinking this way. She was letting herself fall for Peter Dalton.

Eager to see Ashley, Peter hurried to Ida and Cecil's house late the next morning. Her acceptance of his peace offering made him feel better, but her announcement that she'd contacted her dad about the housing issue weighed on his mind. What had she said to her father about Peter's involvement in the situation? He didn't want to be part of a bad report, but there wasn't much he could do about it.

Parking his SUV on the incline of the narrow street, he saw that the workers had finished replacing the floorboards on the porch. They'd scraped away the old paint on the siding and were ready to start painting. He gathered the crew together, including the campus minister who'd accompanied the group.

Peter talked briefly, giving them instructions about where to start and how to paint the exterior of the house. He assigned everyone a spot, opened paint cans and passed out paintbrushes. A dramatic transformation began to take place as they covered the exterior with a fresh, bright coat of white paint.

While Peter checked their progress, he discovered the faded black shutters lying across a couple of sawhorses. He looked around for a can of black paint without success. When he saw Drew and Brandon working on the back porch, Peter joined them. "Hey, guys, have you seen any black paint?"

Drew laid his paintbrush on the nearby paint can and picked

up a can from a box. "Look at this. It says 'Blackgreen.' What kind of color is that?"

"Let's take a look." Peter pried open the lid with a screwdriver and looked at the dark liquid inside. "It looks almost black. I think this is supposed to be for the shutters. Thanks, guys, I'll check with Ida."

After Peter used a paint stick to gather a sample of the paint, he entered the house in search of Ida. He found her exclaiming over the remarkable change in the room where Ashley and several young women were taking the masking tape off the baseboards. When Ida saw Peter, she rushed over to him.

Looking up at him, she made a wide sweeping motion with one hand. "Doesn't it look wonderful?"

"Absolutely." Peter's gaze found Ashley's as she wadded up a long piece of masking tape into a ball. "You do good work."

"Thanks." She gave him a shy smile and continued to remove more masking tape. "We're ready to start the next room."

"Great!" He turned to Ida. "Miss Ida, do you like this paint for your shutters? It's called Blackgreen."

"Looks black to me, but let's show it to Cecil. Follow me." Ida led him to the kitchen where Cecil sat at the kitchen table.

Peter showed Cecil the paint. "Will this color work for your shutters?"

Grinning, Cecil nodded. "Good."

"Thanks for the input." Peter glanced over at Ida, then back at Cecil. "Are you supervising the cookie-making queen?"

Still grinning, Cecil nodded again. "Good cookies."

"That's for sure. Well, I'd better get busy on those shutters." As Peter left the kitchen, he took in the way Cecil looked at Ida. Love radiated from his eyes.

The man depended on Ida's help for everything, and she was there for him. Peter realized they epitomized the "in sickness and in health" part of marriage. He was getting a firsthand look at people who stayed together even when tragedy struck.

He was seeing another example of true love. His parents had it. His brothers had found it, despite the cancer and war wounds that had threatened their lives. Now he could see love was more important than anything money could buy. And more often than he'd like to admit, when he thought of love, he was thinking about Ashley.

When she wasn't around, he missed seeing her. Passing the room where she worked a paint roller up and down the wall, he was tempted to stop, but he forced himself not to linger. He was having enough trouble keeping her off his mind without watching her paint. As he hurried past, something hit him in the back of the head. He turned around as giggles filled the air. A big ball of masking tape lay at his feet.

He stooped and picked it up. "So who has the good aim?"

More giggling accompanied looks of innocence. Moving into the room, he tossed the ball of tape from one hand to the other. "Does anyone want to confess?"

Ashley raised her hand. "I wanted to get your attention."

You already have my attention. "Why?"

"Did you get all your office work done?"

He nodded. "I did. Why?"

"Just checking in case there's something I should do."

"So you had to hit me in the head with a ball of tape to get my attention? A 'Hey, Peter' wouldn't do?"

"I wasn't sure. You looked so intent as you rushed by."

"Got lots on my mind. I went to see our next four projects. The house we have scheduled for next week is in worse shape than I thought, so I ordered more supplies and made arrangements for the plumbing work. We may have to reschedule some of the other houses if this next one takes more than a week to complete."

Frowning, Ashley stopped pulling off the tape and motioned

for Peter to follow her into another room. When she stopped, she turned and looked at him. "Will that affect my schedule?"

"It shouldn't. We'll use the groups on whichever house is ready. If we get behind, I'll contact the homeowners and let them know about the change in the schedule to make sure it'll work for them."

"I'm glad you're here to deal with schedule changes."

"And I'm thankful you're arranging the evening activities like the devotional thing tonight. Definitely not my expertise."

"Then it's a good thing we have each other. I might have gone into a bit of a panic mode if the scheduling didn't work out like we planned."

"You in a panic? I didn't think you ever panicked."

"Why would you say that?"

"Because you're a—"

"Missionary." Shaking her head, she narrowed her gaze. "I told you not to make me out to be this perfect person who never worries and always remembers to rely on God."

"I keep forgetting. You seem perfect to me." He couldn't believe he'd said that, although he was beginning to realize he was thinking of her as perfect in a lot of ways. He liked the challenge she presented. She kept him on his toes and his best behavior. How often lately had he caught himself thinking about everything from her cute freckled nose and the way she scrunched it up when she was thinking hard to her peaceful expression when she prayed in church?

"I think you're exaggerating."

He laughed as he tried to recover from revealing too much about his growing feelings for the little missionary lady. "Maybe you're right, especially since you don't know how to keep from getting paint in your hair."

"What?" She grabbed her ponytail and tried to look at it.

"You can't see it." Stepping closer, Peter reached over and picked up several strands of Ashley's hair and let them slide through his fingers. "Blue streaks and speckles show up very well in those new highlights."

"Oh, no. What will I do?"

"You've never painted before?"

"No. Never."

"It's water-based paint. It'll come out when you wash it." Laughing, he pulled a few strands between his thumb and index finger. Little splatters of the paint came off on his finger, and he showed it to her. "See. I even got some out now."

"So it'll really come out?" She gazed up at him, her amber eyes glowing with a look he couldn't quite decipher, b. made his pulse race.

"Yeah." Unable to tear his gaze away from hers, he was standing so close he could kiss her. Which wouldn't be a wise move. He swallowed hard.

"Oh, good." She quickly turned away, saving him from himself. "I'll have to be more careful."

"I guess you will." He turned to go, thinking he was the one who needed to be more careful. Careful not to do something stupid—like kiss the boss's daughter.

Saturday evening after a week of hard work, the entire volunteer group gathered on Cecil and Ida's front porch for a photograph to commemorate their effort. Smiling broadly, Ashley stood in between Peter and Ida as flashes of light accompanied the clicking sound of camera shutters. The photographer made some humorous remarks in order to elicit smiles from the group while he took several photos. Standing so close to Peter brought to mind all of the things she'd begun to like about him—all of the ways he made her heart flutter.

After the photo session, Ashley tried to push aside her thoughts about Peter. She headed toward the backyard, where a local caterer was setting up to serve a meal.

Peter fell into step beside her. "Well, what do you think? We've made it through the first week, and the house sparkles. Ida and Cecil are ecstatic."

"I know. Thanks to God. He's made it all possible." Despite Ashley's disconcerting thoughts about Peter, she figured his presence on this project was part of God's plan, too.

Peter nodded. "And thanks to you for reminding me that this is all about God, not about our accomplishments."

"I'm not trying to take anything away from the kids who helped this week, but with this amateur in charge of half the operation, I place its success with God."

"You hardly seem like an amateur to me."

"Even after the housing misstep?"

"You handled it, didn't you?"

"I guess if you call having my dad bail me out handling it, then yes."

"We all have to get help from other people from time to time. It's good business sense. When you don't know the answer, you find someone who does. No one does anything by themselves."

"You're right. That's why I like to rely on God."

"Speaking of business sense." Peter pulled some papers out of the portfolio he carried in one hand. "I've got evaluation forms right here. We should hand them out tonight."

"Yes, I'm glad you're the businessman who remembers stuff like this."

"But you remembered to give God the credit."

"We need to do both. Thank God and thank the kids. They were great this week." Ashley held out one hand. "I'll help you pass them out."

Pulling his cell phone out of his pocket, Peter glanced at it, then shoved the whole stack of papers into her out-stretched hand. "I'll let you do this. There's a reporter who's going to meet me out front in about five minutes. He wants to talk to me about the project. That'll give us a little free publicity."

"He should talk to Ida, too."

"Good idea. I'll see you when I finish up."

While Ashley was handing out the forms, Jessica and Libby came rushing up to her in their normal exuberant manner.

"Hey, Ashley," Jessica said as Ashley handed her a form. "We've got a favor to ask you."

"What's that?" Ashley hoped it was something she could do.

Jessica paused for a moment and exchanged a look with Libby. "Well, we were just talking with some of the college kids and they're—"

Libby jumped in before Jessica could finish. "They're going to Amicalola Falls tomorrow after church, and we want to go with—"

"But Mom says we can't go unless you and Peter go, too." Jessica interrupted as the two teens tried to talk over each other.

"Will you go?" Libby asked, her eyes wide as she anticipated Ashley's answer.

Ashley's mind spun with the request. "Can you give me more details—like who all's going and how?"

"Sure." Jessica explained the trip. "Will you do it?"

"I'll talk with your mom and Peter."

Jessica handed Ashley her cell phone. "You can talk to my mom now."

Ashley stared at the phone for a moment, then handed it back to Jessica. Were the two girls trying to push her and Peter together by getting them to go on this trip? She wasn't exactly opposed to the idea, but she cautioned herself against getting too enthusiastic about it. "After I talk to Peter, I'll discuss it with your mom, okay?"

"Let's find Peter." Jessica started off across the yard.

Reaching out, Ashley stopped Jessica. "He's busy talking with a reporter. After he's done, I'll talk to him."

"Will he be done soon? Drew wants us to find out tonight." Jessica bit her bottom lip as she stared at Ashley.

Ashley took in the angst evident in Jessica's words and expression. "So this is all about being with Drew?"

Jessica sighed. "Yes, I like him a lot."

"But you barely know him."

"So I want to get to know him better. There was this connection from the first time we met. You know what I mean?" Jessica shrugged. "And Libby and Brandon have hit it off, too."

"I understand. I'll talk to Peter and your mom before the evening's over."

"Thanks." Jessica gave Ashley a hug. "I'll tell Drew."

Before Ashley could say another word the two teens sprinted across the lawn toward the group of college kids engaged in a game of Frisbee. As she watched them play, she contemplated Jessica's question about the instant connection. Was that what she'd felt the day Peter had picked her up from the airport?

There was something going on between her and Peter. Even with her earlier prejudiced view of him, she'd felt the attraction. She was feeling it every day while they worked side by side. Did he share the same connection, or was it only on her part? How could she figure that out?

"Are we ready to eat?" Peter's voice sounded behind her.

Her heart took a little leap as she turned toward him. Thankfully, he couldn't read minds. "In about ten minutes. They're still setting up. How did it go with the reporter?"

"Super! Thanks for the tip about having him talk to Ida. Cecil even got a word in, but Ida's the star of the article. She made the feature reporter's day with her wit and wisdom."

"When will the story be in the paper?"

"Next week."

"Would you like to play chaperone on a trip to Amicalola Falls?"

"When?"

"Tomorrow after church." Ashley quickly went on to explain Jessica and Libby's request.

Peter glanced in the direction of the Frisbee game, then back at Ashley. "Isn't the campus minister going?"

"No, half the kids are going back to Atlanta with him. The rest are taking this side trip before they head back. And Jessica and Libby want to go. In case you hadn't noticed, Jessica has her eye on Drew."

"Oh, I get it. Teenage crushes."

"If that's what you want to call it."

"Okay. Sounds like it could be fun. I'm in if you are."

"I want to talk with Teresa first to make sure she's on board with the idea."

"Good thinking." Peter pulled his cell phone from his pocket. "Let's call her now."

"Do you have the number?"

"Yep. Got it programmed in." He pressed the appropriate keys, then handed her the phone. "I'll let you talk."

Ashley took the phone and tried not to speculate about why he had the Weavers' number programmed into his phone. Was he thinking about calling her there? *Don't try to make this personal*.

After a couple of rings, Teresa answered the phone. Ashley explained the reason for her call and spent several minutes discussing the trip. After she finished the conversation, she handed the phone back to Peter.

"Are we going?"

Ashley nodded. "Teresa was very thankful. She and Buddy have to make a trip to Atlanta tomorrow afternoon to visit her aunt, who's in a nursing home. Otherwise they would've gone with the girls."

"I'm guessing those girls will be excited not to have their parents tagging along."

"Probably."

"I'm looking forward to the trip." Peter shook his head. "You know, I've lived in Atlanta almost my whole life, and I never bothered to visit this area. I'm glad this situation forced me to discover the beauty of the lakes and mountains. Maybe we can plan a trip to some area attraction every Sunday afternoon. What do you think?"

"We can work on it. Looks like the food's ready." Ashley headed toward the table and tried to figure out whether to be happy or disappointed with Peter's request. She really wanted him to look forward to the trip because he would be with her, but it seemed his thoughts weren't about her. When had she let herself think Peter would ever have an interest in her? Maybe that first day in the airport when he'd smiled at her and she'd been powerless to keep her pulse from racing.

Chapter Thirteen

The winding road clung to the side of the mountain as Peter negotiated the curves with his SUV. These twists and turns were nothing compared to those his mind had taken about Ashley in the past few weeks. She had him tied in knots with her sweetness and her honest way of looking at everything. He was losing his battle not to care too much about her. Maybe today would help him sort things out. But was that going to happen when they weren't alone?

Murmurs from Jessica, Libby, Drew and Brandon mixed with an occasional trill of laughter from one of the girls filled the otherwise quiet interior of his vehicle. He glanced at Ashley, who was studying brochures about Amicalola State Park. Peter forced himself to focus on the road as he followed the gray SUV driven by one of the other college students in the group.

"Tell me about the house we're fixing next week. You said it was in bad shape." Ashley's comment came out of the blue and nearly made him jump.

"Yeah. Most of the paint on the outside is gone, but that saves some time because we won't have to do as much scraping. Some pieces of the clapboard siding are missing. They also need more insulation, so I've put in an order for that, too."

"Have you met the people who own the house?"

"Yes. An older couple, about the same age as Ida and Cecil. Is there some reason you're asking?"

"No, just curious. I should meet them, too. Would you include me next time you visit a project?"

He'd left her out again, and she was reminding him in her quiet, polite way. She never failed to put him on the spot with a reasonable request to include her. Why hadn't he thought about it? He should have the procedure figured out by now. One of these days he was going to get it right.

The turn signal on the vehicle up ahead started to blink, taking Peter's attention away from Ashley. "We're almost there."

Ashley turned to the backseat. "I'm sure glad y'all invited us to go along. I've been reading about the falls and the park. Just think, near here is the beginning of the Appalachian Trail, which goes all the way into Maine. I wonder what it would be like to hike the whole thing."

"I'll leave that to someone else." Peter chuckled.

After they turned onto the road leading into the park, they stopped and paid the entry fee, then found parking at the visitor center and went inside to pick up a map.

Peter looked over the group. "Okay, what does everyone want to do? There are a number of trails for hiking, or we can take the stairs that go to the top of the falls."

"I think we should climb the stairs to the top," Ashley said.

"How many stairs are there?" Libby asked.

Ashley glanced through her brochures. "About six hundred to get to the top of the falls." She looked up. "That's a lot, but that won't stop me."

"Is that a challenge?" Peter asked, forgetting that they weren't the only ones on this trek.

"If you want to make it one." Ashley turned her attention to the others. "What do y'all think?"

Some of the girls looked at each other as if they weren't sure. Then Peter caught the looks on Jessica's and Libby's faces. They didn't seem too enthused about the prospect. Did that mean Peter and Ashley couldn't make the climb because they had to keep an eye on the girls?

"I say we take Ashley's challenge and climb to the top," Drew said. "We can't let these old folks show us up, can we?"

Turning to Ashley, Peter laughed. "Do you think he's talking about us?"

"Speak for yourself," Ashley said.

"Now I know I have to go to the top to prove I'm not one of the old folks."

After Drew agreed to go, the others decided they could make the climb, too. Starting at the visitor center, they followed a broad path that eventually ran beside a creek. Along the way, they came to a reflecting pool, where some folks relaxed while they sat on the edge and dipped their feet in the water.

After they passed the pool, they meandered up the path as it continued to run alongside the creek. A hardwood forest covered the hillsides surrounding the falls. Ashley snapped pictures as she went. Her obvious delight touched Peter's heart.

Suddenly, she grabbed his arm and pointed to the forested area opposite the creek. She whispered, "Look. Do you see the three deer?"

Peter peered into the wooded area as the others stopped and looked. Keeping his voice quiet, he said, "Yes, I see them."

Ashley began taking photos. Seemingly unafraid, the deer didn't move but continued to nibble on the low branches. After she finished, she turned to Peter. "I can't believe they just stood there. That is too cool. Let me show you these."

Peter looked at the digital photos. Her proximity was making it difficult for him to concentrate on them. Several of the others crowded around to look at the digital images, too.

While he stood there, he wished these other people would disappear and leave him and Ashley by themselves. He was going to have to make a time to be alone with her. Should he ask her for a date? He could, but the same old doubts crowded his mind.

What had happened to the confident man who never hesitated to ask a woman out? He'd come face-to-face with Ashley Hiatt, and she'd made him care about missions, about his spiritual life and about her. Asking her for a date meant more than having a beautiful companion for an evening out. They worked together, and she was still his boss's daughter. If the relationship went sour, there could be bad repercussions. Was he brave enough to take that step—a step that might put him in quicksand?

Peter let those questions roll through his mind as the group finished looking at Ashley's photos and resumed their trek to the stairway that would take them to the top of the falls. Up ahead the water tumbled down the rocky mountainside.

Walking beside him, Ashley leafed through a brochure. "It says here the water falls seven hundred and twenty-nine feet down the mountain." She stopped and took another picture. "It's beautiful, isn't it?"

"Yeah." Peter couldn't help thinking Ashley was beautiful. He was beginning to realize how much he looked forward to seeing her every day. He admired the way she encouraged people, how she made everyone feel important and how she wasn't afraid to try something new. Even while she admitted not always understanding everything, she forged ahead. She even tried to understand him. Maybe that was capturing his heart, too.

Peter and Ashley dawdled at the back of the group. Having her beside him gave him a sense of happiness. It had been a long time since any woman had made him feel the way Ashley did. Images of her filled his mind. He could still see her with paint in her hair, singing with her guitar during the devotional and savoring a mustard-covered hot dog like it was a gourmet meal. What new images would make him plunge into this relationship like the water plunging down the mountainside?

When they reached the first observation platform, the group halted. Ashley took more pictures while Peter surveyed the zigzag configuration of staircases leading to the top of the falls. He took a chance and put an arm around Ashley's shoulders in what he hoped would appear as a friendly gesture. "Are you going to push this old man to the top?"

She laughed. "No, you have to make it under your own power. Are you ready?"

Enjoying the sound of Ashley's laughter, Peter turned to the others. "Okay. Here we go."

As they climbed, Peter came to the conclusion that he wasn't in as good shape as he thought he was. Stair-climbing in the real world was different than in the gym. He was glad to catch his breath on the bridge while Ashley took more photos of the falls, as well as photos of everyone on the trip. When she finished, they resumed their ascent. After another four hundred and twenty-five stairs and numerous rest stops, they stood at the top of the waterfall.

"We made it!" Ashley immediately started taking more photos.

Jessica frowned and pointed to a parking lot near the falls overlook. "You mean we could've driven up here?"

"Looks that way." Peter smiled wryly. "But the exercise did us good."

Ashley chuckled. "Yeah, he's not complaining, and he's a lot older than you."

"Is that some kind of backhanded compliment?" Peter wrinkled his brow.

"Take it however you'd like." She continued snapping photos of everyone.

"I think you're having too much fun with that camera." Peter slowly approached her. "What do you think, gang? Should we take away her camera?"

A chorus of "yes" filled the air. Peter reached out to grab the camera, but Ashley managed to dodge him as she stepped away, still snapping photos. As he got closer, she took more pictures of him. Just before he reached her, she took off in a sprint, but she couldn't outrun his long strides.

When he caught her, he gently wrapped his arms around her. She stopped. When he let go, she turned to face him. The camera fell from her hands and hung from the strap around her neck. Her face was flushed as she gazed up at him, her amber eyes full of mischief.

His heart raced from the chase and holding her in his arms. If it weren't for the onlookers, he'd have pulled her close and kissed her. Instead, he lifted the camera from around her neck and started taking her picture. At first she stood with her hands on her hips and frowned at him.

"That pose isn't going to look very good in the photos." Peter continued to take snapshots.

"Oh, you want me to pose. Okay." She gave him a cheesy grin, then made a silly face and finally struck several exaggerated poses imitating fashion models. "Will those do?"

Chuckling, Peter shook his head. "Wait until you see them."

She stopped clowning and gave him a very somber look. "One nice thing about digital photography is being able to delete."

"Oh, so you think you're going to delete the silly photos of you?" Peter turned to the others and held the camera high in the air. "What do you think? Should we confiscate her camera so she can't delete?"

Another loud chorus of agreement and applause filled the air. Other nearby park visitors voiced their approval of Peter's suggestion and chuckled at the group's antics.

"Do you think this is fair? You're much bigger than I am. Besides getting the whole group to gang up on me, you're even getting strangers to take your side." She tried to maintain her frown but finally started laughing helplessly and held out one hand. "If you give me my camera, I promise I won't take any more pictures."

"Oh, no." Peter wagged a finger at her. "You can't fool me with sweet talk. I'll keep the camera until after we upload the photos. Then you can delete all you want."

Ashley shrugged. "Okay. Doesn't bother me. Who cares about the silly photos anyway?"

I do, Peter wanted to tell her, but he kept quiet. The joke was more on him than on her. While he'd held her in his arms, even in a playful way, she'd found her way around his defenses and made him forget about that caution sign that flashed in his brain every time a woman got too close to his heart. He was in much more trouble than he thought.

As Ashley made the trek to the bottom of the falls, she sensed something different about Peter's attention to her. Ever since he'd first put an arm around her just before they started their ascent, she'd wondered what he was thinking. A fluttery feeling had churned in her stomach during the whole trip. His playful actions involving the camera made her hopes soar. Did she dare believe he might have an interest in her that went beyond their working relationship? The thought scared her as much as it excited her.

Did love sometimes turn rational people into folks who did silly things? Maybe like the way her dad had been acting around Charlotte. Ashley hadn't thought much about that relationship in the few weeks she'd been gone.

During the descent, Jessica, Libby and the college students raced down the stairs ahead of them. Peter and Ashley brought up the rear much as they had on the way up. Occasionally, Peter went a few steps ahead and snapped her picture.

"Why are you taking more photos of me? Don't you have enough already?"

"I want to be sure you have a lot of memories of your trip. When you're the one taking the photos, you're never in them. So now you have some of both."

"Don't you think this would be a good time to give my camera back to me?"

Grinning, Peter patted the camera now hanging from the strap around his neck. "No. I wouldn't want anything to happen to any of the photos we've taken today."

"Oh, sure." She rolled her eyes. "You really want to protect those pictures."

"I do."

She narrowed her gaze. "How soon do I get my camera back?"

"As soon as the photos are uploaded onto a computer."

"My computer or yours?"

"Either one. We can do it together."

"Somehow that still doesn't make me feel better."

He draped an arm around her shoulders. "You're too suspicious. My intentions are completely honorable."

Her heart racing, Ashley wished she knew exactly what his intentions were regarding the photos *and her*. When they reached the reflection pool, a number of the kids took off their shoes and sat along the edge with their feet in the water.

Peter glanced at Ashley. "You want to stick your feet in the water, too?"

"Not really."

"Me neither. Let's sit over here." He led her to a nearby picnic area.

Ashley sat on the bench and leaned her back against the table. Peter sat next to her and did the same, stretching his long legs out in front of him. They remained quiet while they watched the activity of dozens of people, young and old, who wandered through the area.

With the lack of conversation, Ashley's mind ran rampant with questions. What did Peter's actions mean? Was the way he teased and touched her today the way he treated all of the women he knew? How should she react? What did her feelings mean?

She'd never had a serious relationship with a man. Could this be love? Was her eagerness to see him every day part of falling in love? Was the way her heart beat faster when she saw him part of that, too? Or were these feelings only physical attraction she couldn't help because Peter, a very handsome and charismatic man, attracted women without trying? How was she supposed to know? She had nothing in her life with which to compare these feelings. She was definitely not a woman with a wealth of knowledge about men.

"Looks like the kids are headed our way." Standing, Peter glanced back in her direction.

Ashley looked at her watch. "I suppose the Atlanta group needs to hit the road about now."

"That would be my guess." He held out a hand to her.

She placed her hand in his, and he pulled her up from the bench. "Thanks," she said, trying to not read anything into his assistance.

She watched Jessica, Drew, Libby and Brandon as they approached. The way the couples looked at each other, touched, laughed and talked together was a clear sign they had romantic feelings for each other. But there were no clear signs with Peter. All of her perceptions were like someone groping through the dark. If only he would give her an obvious indication of his true feelings toward her, then she wouldn't keep second-guessing her own emotions.

When the group reached the parking lot, Peter immediately

unlocked his SUV and opened the door for Ashley. He put her camera in its case and stashed it in the back. "Your camera will be safe back there."

"You mean out of my reach."

"That, too." He grinned.

They waited patiently while Jessica and Libby bid goodbye to Drew and Brandon, as well as the others in the group. The reluctance of the two couples to leave each other showed on their faces.

Peter leaned across the console toward Ashley. "Ah, young love. It can be so painful."

"I suppose."

Was Peter speaking from experience? Had he been hurt by young love? Or was he only making an observation? What would Peter say if he knew she'd never come close to being in love until she'd gotten to know him?

Finally, the goodbyes ended, and Peter drove back along the winding highway. Ashley tried not to let the questions roll through her mind while she listened to Jessica and Libby talk about their plans to visit Drew and Brandon over the summer.

After the girls fell silent, Ashley wondered what she was going to do about her feelings for Peter. He'd sparked an interest in her the first day she came home, but now that little spark was more like a full-fledged blaze. If she didn't get it under control, it could rage like a forest fire that devastated the beauty of the forests covering the hillsides. Letting things get out of hand might lead to an emotional tinderbox that could ignite and destroy her life. *Lord, help me to understand my feelings for Peter and know how to deal with them.*

When they arrived back in town, Peter glanced over at Ashley. "Do you want to grab a bite to eat?"

"Sounds good." Ashley turned to the girls in the back. "Do you want to come, too, since your parents aren't home yet?"

"Sure," they chorused.

"Let's go to the Mexican place across from the lake, okay?" Ashley looked at Peter for approval.

"Yeah. Let's go there. The food's really good," Jessica said before Peter could reply.

"Is the service fast?" Peter asked. "We have to be at the church by seven to meet the new work groups."

"Usually."

"Okay, Mexican it is."

The restaurant was nearly full, but they got a table by the window that looked out on the lake and surrounding mountain peaks. They perused their menus and put in their order. Lively conversation and mariachi music accompanied their delicious meals, and they finished in time to make it to the church to greet the newcomers.

The workers for the week consisted of another group of college kids and two college professors and their wives. After Ashley paired them with the families who were providing their lodging, Peter drove to the Weavers' house.

"Are your parents home yet?" Peter asked.

"Probably not, but we have a key to the house." Jessica gathered her things and stepped out of the SUV. "Thanks for taking us today."

"Yeah. We really appreciate it." Libby joined her sister on the lawn. "Are you coming, Ashley?"

"No, she has to go to the office. I'll bring her back when we're done," Peter said.

"See you later," the girls chorused as they hurried to the front door.

Ashley glared at Peter. "So you're ordering me to go to the office?"

Peter grimaced. "I did it again. Made plans without asking. Although we did talk about uploading your photos."

"We did. So you want to do that now?" Ashley couldn't help smiling.

"Yeah. Then you can have your camera back."

"Okay."

A few minutes later, he parked in front of the office and re-trieved the camera. He unlocked the door and switched on the lights. Cool quietness greeted them.

After connecting the camera to his computer, he turned it on. "I'm going to upload the photos onto my computer. After I'm done, you can put them on yours, too."

"You'll have to show me how." Ashley sat at her desk and turned on her computer.

"No problem." While the photos loaded, he gazed at her from across the room. "I had a good time today."

His statement hung in the air as if it wasn't complete—like he wanted to say something more. Or maybe he was waiting for her to agree. Possibly she was imagining things. Being alone with Peter was wreaking havoc on her mind, especially after the crazy thoughts that had hiked through her brain today.

"Yeah, it was fun, even though I came away with my legs feeling like spaghetti."

"That makes two of us." Laughing, he turned back to the monitor on his desk. "You want to look at these or put them onto your computer first?"

"Does this mean I can have my camera back?"

"Absolutely."

"I'll put them on my computer before we look at them."

"Okay." He unplugged the cord from his computer. Without getting out of the chair, he rolled it across the room until he was next to her. He connected the camera to her computer, and in minutes the photos were uploaded. "Ready to take a look?"

"Yes." Ashley clicked the mouse to start a slide show.

As the photos appeared one by one on the screen, Peter

leaned closer. Ashley's pulse quickened as their shoulders brushed. She gave him a surreptitious glance. He was totally absorbed in the pictures. Then he chuckled, and she returned her gaze to the screen. Her image appeared. One silly pose after another popped up for them to see.

"Do we have to look at these?" Letting out a loud sigh, she gripped the arms of her chair.

"Why not? I think they're pretty entertaining."

"I don't."

"You're the one who posed."

"Yeah, but I thought I'd delete them."

"You can do that any time you want."

"But they'll still be on your computer."

"True." He grinned.

"Just exactly what are you going to do with those?"

He pressed his lips together as if he was thinking hard. "Maybe print them out and use them to scare away burglars from my condo."

"Quit teasing me."

"I can't. You're fun to tease." Peter turned to look at a photo of Jessica and Drew. "Well, what do you think? Will Jessica and Libby find some new love interests in this week's group?"

"That's a cynical thing to say."

"No. Just reality."

"They spent the afternoon with Drew and Brandon, and they're making plans to see each other through the summer. Do you still think the girls will find some other boys to latch on to this week?"

While the slide show continued, Ashley stared at him and wondered whether that was his view of romance and the dating game. Maybe that was why he never dated someone for more than a few months.

Surely there was something more to his inability to have a

long-term relationship than the feeling that one woman would do until a new one came along. That kind of thinking didn't fit with the man she'd come to know over the past few weeks. If that was his attitude, what was she doing letting herself fall in love with him?

"They're young. Their attention spans are short."

Frowning, Ashley shook her head. "My mom and dad were high school sweethearts. Just because a person's young doesn't mean they don't know what love is."

"Okay, I'll agree some young relationships do last, but you have to admit those are few and far between."

"You're not young. So what's your excuse for finding a new woman every time you turn around?"

Peter rocked back in his chair and crossed his arms. "Ouch! You sure know how to hurt a guy. An old Casanova, is that how you see me?"

Seeing the hurt on his face, she hung her head and wished she could take back her tactless words. What had possessed her to blurt out her unkind thoughts? "I'm so sorry. I don't think you're old, just older than Jessica and Libby. And dating a lot of different women doesn't make you a Casanova."

"There's one thing I like about you. At least I know where I stand."

Still hanging her head, Ashley couldn't look him in the eye. All of the foolish thoughts she'd had about Peter this afternoon must have short-circuited her brain. "Who you date is none of my business. Please forgive me."

Chapter Fourteen

Peter's heart ached. Despite Ashley's apology, she obviously didn't have a very high opinion of him. He desperately wanted to change that. He reached over and touched her arm. "Ashley, I forgive you, but you don't have anything to apologize for."

Slowly she lifted her head and stared at him. "But I didn't have to say anything."

"Yes, but it's better that I know what you think."

Ashley shrugged. "I suppose, but it really is better to say nothing if you can't say something nice."

There she was again—getting right to the point. Could he be as honest as she was? "True, but I like your honesty, and you've touched something deep in here." He placed a fist over his heart.

"What do you mean?"

What did he mean? He was still trying to figure out his feelings. Was he ready to push aside old fears and make an effort to convince her that he was worth taking a chance on?

He'd made up his mind this afternoon to ask her for a date. Now he had to prove himself worthy of her time. If he wanted her to have a different opinion of him, he'd probably have to tell her about his broken engagement. Maybe the story would persuade her that he wasn't such a bad guy after all.

He took a deep breath. "My feelings for you go beyond friendship. That probably doesn't mean much, since you think I date women like I'm trying out the flavor of the month." He paused to figure out how to go on. Thankfully, she didn't say anything. "Remember when you asked me why I was still single?"

She still didn't speak, just nodded her head.

"Well, my senior year in college I got engaged to a girl I started dating my sophomore year. We planned to get married at the end of August the summer after our graduation. I'd gotten a job with Hiatt Construction, and she was going to go to law school at Emory. Everyone thought we were the perfect couple, but it was all a lie."

Ashley reached over and touched him on one arm. "I can tell it hurts you to talk about it. You don't—"

"Yes, I do. This is as much for me as it is for you. I've never talked about this with anyone. It's been over fifteen years, and it's time I did."

"Okay." Ashley's voice came out in a raspy whisper.

Already feeling better, Peter covered her hand with his. "Jenn, my fiancée, had a ten-week summer internship with a law firm back in Chicago, where we'd gone to college. She stayed there while I went to Atlanta to start my job." Pausing, he glanced away.

"Really, Peter, you don't have to tell me."

Averting her gaze again, he took both of her hands in his and gently squeezed them. "It's okay."

"If you say so." She gave him a weak little smile.

His heart thumping, he swallowed a lump in his throat. "Anyway, over the Fourth of July, I flew to Chicago to surprise her, and the surprise was on me."

"What happened?"

"She had eloped with one of my fraternity brothers."

Ashley's face registered shock. "She eloped without breaking your engagement?"

Peter laughed bitterly. "She broke the engagement. She just forgot to tell me."

"How'd you find out?"

"She was sharing an apartment with some girls who didn't know me. When I told them I was Jenn's fiancé, the look on their faces was total panic. They didn't know how to tell me she was in Las Vegas getting married to someone else." Peter let out a harsh breath. "So that's the story."

He got up and walked to the window and gazed out at the nearly empty street. The streetlights were just coming on. The sky was awash in reds. His anger over Jenn's betrayal had made him see red. For a long time, he'd thought he would never get over it. He hoped his story would help Ashley understand why caring about someone scared him—why the thought made him want to run. But he was determined not to run from his feelings this time.

Ashley went to stand beside him. Putting an arm around her waist, he pulled her close. She laid her head against his shoulder. "I'm so sorry that happened. I can't imagine how much it must've hurt."

"That's why I became a serial dater." Turning to face her, he put his hands on her shoulders. She gazed up at him and his pulse raced, heart thudding against his ribcage. She was worth taking another chance on love. "I don't want to do that anymore. I've come to realize over the past few weeks that you're a special woman. Will you give me an opportunity to prove that I'm not a bad risk? Go out with me next weekend."

She nodded, and he pulled her into his arms and held her close for a few minutes. Then he kissed her gently on the lips.

She clung to him, and he felt at home—a feeling he hadn't had in a very long time. This time he hoped this woman wouldn't break his heart.

Weeks later, Ashley put on the new white eyelet top and surveyed herself in the mirror. Would Peter like how she looked? Her stomach churned with anticipation. Even though they'd been dating for over a month now, seeing Peter, even at work, always left her with an overwhelming fluttery feeling.

Jessica stood in the doorway. "I'm so happy you and Peter finally got together. He'll love that outfit."

"Thanks for helping me pick it out."

"Where are y'all going today?"

"On the Blue Ridge Scenic Railway. We're leaving to catch the train after church."

"Y'all have done some cool stuff lately, like that romantic boat ride on Lake Chatuge." Smiling, Jessica clasped her hands together. "Lib and I are going into Atlanta with Mom and Daddy to visit Aunt Jules. Then we get to see Drew and Brandon. I'm so excited."

"Guess we're all in for a great day." Ashley ran a brush through her hair. "I'd better hurry. Peter will be here soon."

"I'd better hurry, too." Jessica ran across the hall to her room.

While Ashley finished getting ready, she couldn't help remembering Peter's comments about Jessica and Libby. Even though everything was wonderful between her and Peter, Ashley sometimes wondered whether their relationship would last beyond the summer. When she heard Peter's voice downstairs, her heart leaped. She shook away the negative thought and hurried down the stairs to meet him.

He smiled when he saw her. "You look pretty. Another new outfit?"

"Yes. Thanks."

Waving to the Weavers, he ushered her out the front door. "Jessica and Libby have made you a fashion plate."

"I knew you'd say that." She flashed him a perturbed look. "Just because I get a new outfit doesn't mean I've turned into a fashion plate."

He opened the door for her. "Yes, I know, but I can't help teasing you a little. I'll never forget the day I picked you up from the airport and took you shopping. I wish I'd taken a picture of you in those oversized clothes. You were too cute, and the expression on your face was priceless when you had to admit you should've tried them on."

When he settled in the driver's seat, she pretended to be annoyed. "Have you had enough laughter at my expense?"

Laughing again, he leaned over the console and gave her a quick kiss. "I adore you."

Smiling at him, Ashley felt the warmth of Peter's words, but she was reluctant to express her own feelings.

During church, she tried to listen to the sermon, but her mind constantly wandered to the man sitting beside her. She wondered why she had a hard time telling him how she felt.

Saying what she thought was usually so easy, but she was beginning to see she was as vulnerable to hurt as Peter.

Ever since her mom died, she'd been afraid to get close to anyone, sometimes even her dad, whom she loved dearly. Could she finally overcome that with Peter? Could they help each other heal wounds from the past?

Ashley and Peter arrived in Blue Ridge a few minutes before the train was ready to depart. She cast a longing glance at the shops lining the main street near the depot.

"I saw that look." Peter grabbed her hand as they walked to the train.

"What look?"

"At the shops."

She giggled. "I thought I might find something cute for Ida."

"If the shops are still open when we get back, I'll make sure you have time to look. Besides, I believe you can shop when the train stops in McCaysville." He winked at her. "I'm learning what to expect from you."

"Good." Ashley climbed aboard the train and wondered whether she knew what to expect from herself where Peter was concerned.

Ashley settled in her seat in the open-air railcar. A few minutes later the bell on the train clanged and the whistle blew as the engine chugged forward, pulling the train away from the station. As the train started its journey to McCaysville, Georgia, Ashley retrieved her camera from the carrying case and put the strap around her neck.

"I see you're ready to take photos."

"Yes. I should get some good ones."

"You get good ones on every trip. I'm impressed with your photography. Have you ever thought about doing anything with your photos?"

"Like what?"

"Maybe trying to get them published."

Ashley shook her head. "It's just something I enjoy doing. I especially like the digital camera."

"So you've been enticed to indulge in all kinds of electronic gadgets as well as fashion." Peter chuckled.

Ashley sighed. "I know. You've completely corrupted me."

"Maybe not completely. You still only play acoustic guitar." Peter put an arm around her shoulders and pulled her close. "We had another good week, didn't we?"

"We did. I can't believe how fast the summer is going. Labor Day and the end of summer will be here before we know it."

"Yeah, but we've accomplished a lot."

"Praise God."

"Yeah. We can't forget to do that. Thanks for reminding me to give God the credit. You've been good for my spiritual life. You've helped make this mission work a real part of me."

Surprised by Peter's admission, Ashley wasn't quite sure what to say. "Really? Aren't you giving me a little more credit than I deserve?"

"No. I learned that last Sunday after Pastor Rob read those scriptures about how we should encourage each other. Even though you don't realize it, you've done that for me."

"How?"

"Like reminding me to give God the credit."

"But how does that encourage you?"

"Because it makes me think beyond myself and what I'm doing."

"I think you're already doing that. Like helping Tim."

Peter shrugged. "Now you're giving *me* too much credit. Helping Tim was nothing. I enjoyed that."

"You know it's okay to enjoy doing good."

"That 'It's better to give than receive' thing again?"

"Yes, that." Ashley picked up her camera. "I want to get some shots of the Toccoa River."

"I have a feeling you're going to be glued to that camera for the rest of the trip."

"Maybe." Ashley started snapping photos, not wanting to think about Peter's spiritual growth. She should be happy he was putting God in his thoughts and plans, and she was. So what made her uneasy? Her mind chugged around that question like the train chugging along the tracks. Crazy as it was, she saw his admission as one more reason to fall for this man. One more reason to shove aside the fear of sharing her heart with him.

She still cautioned herself not to get too caught up in the romance. Peter Dalton, despite his good qualities, was still a man who had a reputation for short-lived relationships. Even though he'd explained the reason behind this, she still had a niggling doubt that she wasn't the kind of woman who could change that.

Still, she was finding more and more to love about him. She felt as though falling in love with Peter was like jumping out of an airplane and hoping the parachute opened. There was a matchless thrill in falling. She only hoped the landing wouldn't kill her.

The following Friday, Ashley surveyed the house they had started renovating at the beginning of the week. This week had flown by as all the others had. Although the volunteers changed each week, all of the work weeks had fallen into a similar pattern.

Ashley and Peter spent an hour or two each day in the office, but most of the time they worked on the houses. Cookouts, devotions, singing and recreation time filled the evenings. Ida and Cecil's house became an example for the subsequent projects, and Ida continued to provide cookies for the workers. Everything was going well.

Even after her talk with Peter about how fast the weeks had gone, she couldn't believe August was here. School would begin soon. This summer's projects would end, and they would start planning for next year. Where would the projects take them?

As Ashley applied paint to the siding in smooth, even strokes, she thought about Peter's family, who would arrive on Sunday. She looked forward to meeting them, but at the same time, the thought made her nervous. Had Peter told his family that they were dating? She hadn't mentioned it to her father, because, deep in her heart, she feared the relationship might not last.

When her brush ran out of paint, Ashley dipped it into the paint can. As she pressed the brush to the siding, a big drop of paint plopped onto her shoe. Looking around for a rag, she didn't see one. She hurried around the corner of the house to find a rag but stopped short when a beautiful brunette woman emerged from a car and headed in Peter's direction.

When he saw her, he quickly laid his paintbrush on the paint can. He smiled and held out his arms. She gave him a hug, and they immediately fell into an animated conversation.

The paint blob forgotten, Ashley zipped around the corner and returned to her work before Peter or the woman noticed her. Was this one of his old girlfriends? Ashley didn't want to be jealous, but the insidious emotion filled her mind like the caulk she'd used to fill the cracks in the siding. She closed her eyes and tried to push it away—push away the hurt squeezing her heart.

She'd told herself going into this relationship that it might not last, but somehow her heart had never gotten the message. Well, the message should find its way there now. She stroked the paint-brush along the siding with a vengeance. Taking a deep breath, she said a quick prayer. She had to leave her relationship with Peter in God's hands even though she wanted to control the outcome.

While she stewed, her curiosity won out, and she ventured to the corner of the house. As she did, Peter got into a car with the woman. Ashley's heart sank. Where was he going? And who was she?

Trying to talk herself out of a negative attitude, she began painting fast and furiously. She wouldn't let herself cry. She should believe Peter cared for her. He'd never actually said the words "I love you," but everything he'd done in recent weeks told her that he did. So why was he driving off with some other woman?

"Ashley! Ashley!" Jessica ran around the corner, a paint-brush waving in one hand.

Libby followed close behind. "Did you see Rachel Carr? Peter just drove away with her. What is she doing here? Do you and Peter know her?"

Her heart hammering, Ashley listened to the string of questions with a growing sense of uncertainty. "Who's Rachel Carr?"

"You don't know?" Surprise registered on Jessica's face.

"No. Is that the woman Peter left with?"

"Yes. She's a famous actress."

"An actress?"

"Yeah. She's on a TV show and in movies."

"I haven't watched American TV or movies in over five years. I've never seen her." Ashley shook her head as worry crowded her mind. She tried to tell herself she shouldn't be bothered that the man she cared about had ridden off with a beautiful actress. Who was she kidding? It bothered her a lot.

"I hope we get to meet her. Will Peter introduce us?" Libby asked.

Ashley shrugged. "Maybe."

"I hope so." Jessica grinned. "I've never met anyone famous."

"We won't know anything until Peter gets back, so let's get to work."

The girls hurried off as Ashley started painting again. A sick feeling sat like a stone in the pit of her stomach. Was this actress someone he'd dated? Maybe she was going to contribute money to the mission. Famous people often did that.

But how did Peter know her? The questions haunted Ashley. She wished she could slap her fears on the side of the house and paint over them. Hoping she could rid herself of the troubling thoughts, she painted even faster.

"Ashley." She heard Peter's voice from around the corner before she saw him. When he saw her, he smiled. "There you are."

"I've been here all the time. What have you been doing?" Her heart racing, Ashley forced a smile and hoped her question sounded natural, even though she was fighting the green-eyed monster.

Peter motioned to her. "Come with me. I want you to meet my family. They've just arrived."

"This is Friday. I thought they weren't coming until Sunday."

"They decided to come early to go sightseeing."

Family? Was it possible the woman was part of his family? Relief flooded her mind, but she cautioned herself not to jump to any more conclusions. She set down her paintbrush and followed Peter to the edge of the front yard. The woman she'd seen earlier stood beside a tall blond man and a little girl. Another couple, four small children and Peter's parents got out of an SUV and joined them.

Peter grabbed her hand and pulled her forward. "Ashley, I want you to meet my brother, Matt, and his wife, Rachel, and their little girl, Becky. And over here is Wade and his wife, Cassie, and their four, Taylor, Makayla, Jack and Danny." Peter tapped each of the youngsters on the head as he said their names. "And you've met my parents, Gloria and Harold, right?"

"Yes, we met at church before I went to the mission field." Ashley nodded, angry with herself for jumping to ridiculous conclusions about Rachel. Peter's brother was married to the famous actress. Wait until Jessica and Libby found out.

Gloria stepped forward and shook Ashley's hand. "It's good to see you again. Peter told me you had to leave the mission field because of terrorists. How terrible!"

"Yes, it was."

"Mom." Peter took her arm. "Ashley doesn't like to talk about it."

"Oh, okay." Surprise painted Gloria's face as she looked at her son, then back at Ashley. "I'm so sorry, Ashley. I didn't mean to bring up an unpleasant topic."

"Don't worry about it." Ashley waved a hand as if to erase the conversation. Her stomach churning, she tried to hold her smile in place as she shook hands with Peter's father, brothers and their wives and greeted each of the children. What had Peter told them about her? Would they like her? That fluttery feeling settled around her heart again, but she tried to ignore it. "How was your trip?"

"It was a lovely drive. And we're excited to be helping out with the mission work." Gloria turned to the rest of the group. "Now that Peter has given us the key to the place we've rented, we're headed out there. Peter says you're free this evening, so I hope you'll join us for dinner."

Her heart lighter, Ashley smiled. "Thanks. I'd love to."

"We'll see you later." Peter put an arm around Ashley's shoulders as his family returned to their vehicles.

After they left, Ashley turned to Peter. "I think I'd better warn you Jessica and Libby have already recognized Rachel. I hope people won't be bugging her."

"So you know she's an actress?"

"Not until Jessica and Libby clued me in."

"Rachel's used to dealing with fans." Chuckling, Peter walked toward the house. "It still seems weird having a celebrity in the family, especially since I remember Rachel as a little girl." Peter proceeded to tell Ashley about his summer visits to his uncle's farm in South Dakota and how Rachel had tagged along with the brothers and their cousins and how she and Matt eventually fell in love.

Ashley climbed the steps to the porch. "I noticed Matt's injuries. I hope you don't mind my asking about them."

"I don't." Peter followed her back to the spot where she'd been painting. "He was injured by a roadside bomb in Afghanistan several years ago. He almost died." Peter stopped and looked at her. "You should also know Wade has battled Hodgkin's disease."

Ashley placed a hand over her heart. "What a terrible ordeal for your family!"

Peter nodded. "It was tough for my parents."

"That must have all happened while I was on the mission field. If I'd known, I would've prayed for them."

"I know you would've. I'm eager for you to get to know

them." Peter put an arm around her shoulders again and pulled her close. "You're an inspiration to me. Even after seeing how God worked in my brother's lives, it still took you and this mission work to turn my spiritual life around."

His words melted her heart. Gazing up at him, she wanted to slip into his embrace, but this wasn't the proper time or place. "You're always giving me too much credit."

"Then let's give God the credit for bringing you into my life."

Her heart hammering, Ashley smiled. "And you into mine."

He gave her a quick kiss on the cheek. "I'd better get back to work. We wouldn't want to be accused of making out when we're supposed to be working, would we?"

Picking up her paintbrush, Ashley giggled. "No."

After Peter left, Ashley continued painting. His words forced her to acknowledge the need to overcome her doubts about him. Her own insecurities created the problem, not Peter. She was the one who couldn't believe he could actually care for her. The time had come to trust him.

Chapter Fifteen

Before supper that evening, Peter's mother approached him from the other end of the rented lake house deck. The look on her face told him that she was armed with questions. Every time he started dating someone new, she made negative comments. Gazing at the lake, he leaned his forearms on the railing and hoped he was wrong this time.

His mother joined him. "Why aren't you down on the dock with your brothers?"

"I'm waiting for Ashley. She had to run an errand." He braced himself for his mother's quiz.

"Is everything going well with the mission project?"

"Yes."

"What happens after the summer projects are done?"

"Ashley and I will meet with Richard and make an assessment of the summer and make plans for the future."

"So is this a permanent thing?"

"As far as I know."

"And you're happy with that?"

"Yes." Surprisingly, he was. What was his mother getting at?

These weren't the kinds of questions he'd expected. When was she going to start grilling him about Ashley?

"I'm glad." Gloria nodded. "Even though this is a worthy cause, I was afraid the position was all wrong for you."

"I had my doubts, too, but it's been challenging and rewarding."

"Then you and Ashley work well together?"

This was it. Now she was going to pepper him with the questions he'd expected. "We do."

"That's good, since she's your boss's daughter *and* you're dating. Does that ever concern you?"

"A little." Peter hadn't expected that question. He wished she'd just come out and ask what she wanted to know rather than bobbing and weaving around it.

She gave him one of her laser-beam looks. "What do you suppose will happen when you break that girl's heart?"

Peter pushed away from the railing. "Break her heart?"

"Yes. You go out with women as long as you can keep them at a distance."

"You never liked any of them, anyway."

"Ashley's different. She has substance. She's not just a pretty face. And she's not someone you can date, then throw away when it's convenient."

Peter didn't appreciate his mother's appraisal of his dating patterns. "You mean for once you don't think the woman I'm dating is too young, too old, too rich, too poor, too—"

"Peter, enough sarcasm." Gloria sighed. "How serious is your relationship?"

"We're dating." Peter wasn't sure how deep his feelings ran beyond that. His mother was right. He had an abysmal track record with women.

"Just dating? I suspected more than that when you protected

her by telling me she didn't want to talk about her departure from Africa."

"Don't try to read anything into my actions." Even though his mother's interference irritated him, he wanted her approval.

"I think Ashley's a wonderful young woman. Just from what I've seen, it seems to me she's been good for you."

"We have a good time together."

"I'm talking about more than having a good time this summer. One of these days you need to settle down like your brothers. She'd make a good wife, but you're never looking for one."

Peter gritted his teeth to keep from making another sarcastic remark. Instead of discouraging his relationship with Ashley, his mother was actually encouraging it. He cared a lot about Ashley, but he wasn't sure he was in love with her. "Don't try to push me into anything."

"I'm not." Gloria gave him another one of her famous looks. "I just want you to realize what a gem Ashley is, and that you shouldn't be toying with her emotions. If this relationship doesn't last, it could interfere with your job."

"Is this about my love life or my job?"

"Both. I'm only trying to make sure no one gets hurt, especially Ashley."

Peter didn't have a response. "I don't intend to hurt her."

"I hope you know what you're doing."

"I do," Peter said as he saw Ashley walking across the yard. "Ashley, I'm up here."

She turned and waved. "You want me to come up?"

"No. I'll come down."

As Peter turned to go, his mother caught his arm. "As long as you're leaving, tell everyone to come up for dinner. And remember what I've said."

"I'm sure if I forget, you'll remind me." Peter took off before his mother could reply. He hurried down the stairs to meet Ashley. Seeing her lifted his spirits.

She met him at the bottom of the stairs. "Hi. I hope I didn't hold up dinner."

"You're just in time. I'm on my way to the lake to get the others." He put an arm around her shoulders. "I'm glad you're here."

She smiled up at him and his heart soared. Was his mother right? Was Ashley the one for him? "Me, too. I'm eager to get to know your family better."

"Even those rambunctious kids?"

"Especially the kids. Remember, I was a schoolteacher."

As soon as Peter and Ashley reached the dock, the four older children raced toward them. Taylor and Makayla grabbed Peter's hands. They dragged him toward the dock. "Uncle Peter, come see what we caught."

"Okay." He gave Ashley a helpless smile. "See what I mean?"

"I forget." Makayla pointed to Ashley. "What's her name?"

"Ashley."

"Miss Ashley, you come, too." Makayla came back and grabbed her hand.

Soon the children were clamoring around Peter and Ashley as they showed off their fish. He watched her exclaim over them, giving *oohs* and *aahs* at the appropriate times. She was a natural with kids. He loved the way she managed to find common ground with any group, young or old. He was finding too much to like about her. Not willing to examine his feelings more closely, he pushed the thought to the back of his mind.

When the group started back to the house, Makayla grabbed Peter's hand. Ashley walked ahead of them with Taylor and Becky. How had he managed to attract the child that would talk his ear off?

"Uncle Peter, is Ashley your wife?"

"No, she's just my friend." Even as he said it, his mother's words rang through his head.

All through dinner he watched his brothers and their wives. Is that what he wanted for himself? He'd told himself for years that he wouldn't consider marriage again, but Ashley and her cute, quirky ways had made him rethink that position. Could he rid himself of his fears and let himself fall in love with her?

After dinner, everyone went out on the deck to eat dessert. They sat around, talking and laughing as Peter and his brothers told stories about each other.

After Peter regaled them with a story about Wade, he looked over at Ashley. "What have you done to Peter this summer? I've never seen him so relaxed."

Ashley shrugged. "Must be the mountain air."

"I think it might be something else." Wade clapped Peter on the back. "Peter, would you like to explain?"

Standing, Peter grabbed Ashley's hand and pulled her to her feet. "No. We're going for a walk."

Hoots and howls followed them while Peter raced Ashley down the steps. A remark about lovebirds drifted through the air as they walked across the yard.

"Sorry about that. They can get carried away. I don't suppose this is a good time to ask you what you think of my family?"

"Your family's wonderful. It must've been fun to grow up with your brothers." Laughing softly, Ashley snuggled in the crook of his arm as they walked together toward the lake.

"Most of the time," he said as her quiet words and laughter warmed his heart. "But they can be annoying."

"Isn't that what families are for? To annoy us as well as love us?" Ashley laughed again. "I love my dad, but he can make me crazy. You witnessed the driving lessons."

Thinking about his mother, Peter joined the laughter. "There's no doubt. They do both."

When they reached the dock, they walked to the end. The soothing sound of the water as it lapped gently against the dock supports accompanied their footsteps. While the sun slowly slipped behind the clouds dancing on the mountain peaks, Peter and Ashley stood arm in arm.

His heart racing, Peter tried to figure out how he felt about Ashley. His mother's questions had forced him to examine what he intended for this relationship. His heart told him that Ashley was everything he needed. She made him laugh. She challenged him. She made him think beyond himself. But his head was filled with the same old fears. He'd trusted his heart before, and it had failed him.

Ashley motioned toward the western sky. "I love colorful sunsets, and seeing them reflected in the lake makes it that much better. God sure knows how to paint a picture."

"He does." Knowing how much her influence had changed his spiritual life, Peter turned to face her. He couldn't say he loved her, but he could tell her that much. "He's painted me several pictures this summer. Through you, He's given me a new purpose for my life—helping others through this mission work."

"I've learned that, too."

Taking a deep breath, Peter took her hands in his. He gazed into her amber eyes, then pulled her close. His mother's warning rippled through his mind again. If he loved Ashley, wouldn't that love drive out his fears? Maybe time would give him the answer to that question.

A week later, Ashley stood in the yard of the Daltons' rented lake house with Peter's sisters-in-law and his mother and watched him play tag with his brothers and the kids. The mission week with his family had raced by. The Dalton clan had joined in the house painting and repair as well as all the activities from ball games to devotions.

Ashley loved not only Peter, but his family, too. Their love had drawn her into their circle. Did she dare dream that Peter could fall in love with her, marry her and make her a permanent part of this wonderful clan? Sometimes, she was sure he loved her, even though he hadn't said the words, but she also remembered how vehement he'd been about not getting married. Did he still feel that way? Did she have any hope of changing his mind?

The sound of a car door slamming shut made her turn around. Waving, her father walked toward her.

"Daddy, what are you doing here?" Ashley ran to greet him.

Her father gave her a big hug. "Peter's parents invited me for dinner."

"Why didn't you call me?"

Shaking his head, he chuckled. "You're never in the office, and you never turn on your cell."

"I forget."

"I know." Richard chuckled. "I've intended to spend a weekend with you ever since I bought the lake house, but work kept getting in the way. I was beginning to think you were right about my never having time to enjoy the place. But that's all going to change."

"Change how?"

"I'll tell you after I say hello to Gloria and Harold." Her father draped an arm around her shoulders as they moseyed across the yard.

As they approached, Gloria came to greet them. "Richard, I'm glad you could come. Let me introduce you to my daughters-in-law and the grandkids."

Ashley and her father followed Gloria over to the spot where Rachel and Cassie were watching the game of tag.

After the introductions, Richard looked at Gloria. "Is that Harold on the dock?"

"Yes. He's trying out his new fishing rod."

"I'm going down to say hi."

Gloria nodded. "Okay. Don't let him bore you with his fishing tales."

"I won't." Chuckling, Richard turned to Ashley. "Go with me?"

"Sure, Daddy." Ashley fell into step beside her father. "So what are these changes you're going to make?"

Richard slowed his pace. "I know this could come as a shock, but…I'm…I'm getting married."

Ashley stopped and stared at her father. "Married?"

"Yes, to Charlotte. The wedding's going to be in September at the lake house. Please be happy for us."

Laughing, Ashley hugged her father. "Daddy, I'm delighted. My suspicions were right."

"Your suspicions?"

"Yes, when I came home I saw the way the two of you were acting, but I was afraid to ask about it. When did this happen?"

Her dad shook his head. "Slowly, over the past couple of years. At first, when I realized I'd developed feelings for Charlotte, I was afraid of upsetting our friendship and her role as my housekeeper."

"What changed?"

"One Saturday, our pastor urged me to go to the Silver Singles group at church. That's what they call us old singles." Her father chuckled. "I didn't want to go, but they were going to the symphony. So I thought I'd give it a try."

"And Charlotte was there, right?"

"Yes. We enjoyed the evening together, and we started attending the Silver Singles stuff on a regular basis."

"Like dating."

"Oh, no. We weren't dating—just attending church functions." He laughed again. "One day we quit dancing around our feelings, and here we are getting married."

"Why didn't you bring Charlotte with you?"

"Because I wanted to tell you in private, and she's telling her kids tonight, too. Then they're driving up tomorrow."

"Super!" Ashley gave her father another hug.

"I have another announcement to make at dinner."

"About what?"

"The mission project."

"Please tell me now."

"At dinner. Peter needs to be there, too."

"That makes sense."

After Ashley and Richard visited with Harold for a few minutes, the trio made their way to the house.

Throughout the meal, Ashley waited for her dad to make his announcement. What was he going to say about the mission? Surely, they'd fulfilled her dad's objectives, and he would continue to fund the work. She prayed that she wouldn't be disappointed.

While everyone ate dessert, her father pushed his chair back and stood. "I'd like to make an important announcement."

"Go ahead," Harold said.

"I told Ashley when I first arrived, but I wanted to share this news with the rest of you, too." Pausing, Richard glanced around the room. "I'm happy to announce I'll be marrying Charlotte Perdue next month."

Congratulations and applause filled the room. After the commotion died down, Richard glanced around. "That brings me to my next announcement. Because I'm getting married and getting older, I plan to cut back drastically on my work schedule. That means I'll be stepping down as the head of Hiatt Construction."

A murmur rose around the table, and Ashley stifled a gasp. Her dad—stepping down? She couldn't believe it.

When the murmur subsided, Richard gestured around the table. "There'll be a formal announcement next week, but I wanted to share this tonight. Peter's always done whatever I've asked of him, the latest request being this mission project. He's done a great job, and now I'm proud to announce that Peter will take over as head of Hiatt Construction at the beginning of September." Richard glanced at Ashley. "And my daughter will take complete charge of the mission project."

As her dad's words sunk in, Ashley looked at Peter. His smile turned into a wide grin as he stood and shook her father's hand. "Thank you, sir. You don't know what this means to me. I know it'll be a big job to fill your shoes, but you can count on me to do my best and make you proud."

"I know you will."

While everyone congratulated her and Peter, Ashley was dying inside. Somehow she managed to smile while she congratulated Peter. He gave her a hug, but she pulled away when he tried to keep her at his side. She had to get away. While everyone laughed and talked, she escaped to the deck. Leaning against the side of the house, she closed her eyes, fighting back the tears.

When she finally gained control of her emotions, she looked at the lake. The dock, jutting out into the moonlit water, took her back to the night last week when Peter had declared that the mission had given him a true purpose for his life. Now he was abandoning it.

Had he only said those things because that's what he thought she wanted to hear? Would he treat their relationship like the mission work? It was good enough until something better came along. The thought made her sick. Better to find out now rather than to pin her hopes on the dreams she had entertained.

She didn't want to remember his words. She couldn't trust them. His actions told her that he didn't really care about it. He only cared about pleasing her father—something she had witnessed from the beginning.

She'd been so stupid to let her silly heart believe she had a chance to win Peter's love. Peter was all about business. Hiatt Construction held his heart.

The swooshing of the sliding glass door signaled someone else's presence. Taking a deep breath, she looked toward the door.

Peter stepped out. "Ashley, I wondered where you were."

"Just getting some fresh air." She produced a smile. "Congratulations again."

"Thanks."

"You know this means I win," Ashley said, although it didn't feel like winning.

"What are you talking about?"

"You're leaving the mission work. So I win."

His smile faded. "I'm not leaving now."

"At the beginning of September, you are. You'll be going back to Atlanta to the job I suspect you've always wanted."

He stood there, his gaze narrowed, without saying a thing.

"You can't deny it, can you?"

"You're right. I've always wanted this job, but that shouldn't change anything between us."

"It changes everything. Just days ago you told me the mission project was your life, but I see how long that lasted." She swallowed a lump in her throat. "How can I trust someone who tells me one thing but does another?"

"How did I do that?"

"You said you wanted to do mission work."

"Circumstances change. So you have to reevaluate."

"So go back to Atlanta and run Daddy's company. That's what you want to do. Where you want to be."

"I want to be with you." Peter put a hand on her arm.

She ducked away. "If that were true, why would you take the job the minute Daddy offered it to you? You didn't even ask me what I thought."

"I never imagined you'd object."

"The same old Peter—jumping to conclusions about what I think." Ashley narrowed her gaze. "You're just tossing the mission project aside."

"No, I'm leaving it in very capable hands. Yours. That's what your dad wants."

"Don't flatter me."

"It's not flattery. It's the truth. You know how to run it. You don't need me anymore."

"That's right. I'm reevaluating, too. Guess we don't need each other."

"I didn't mean it that way."

Rubbing her forehead, she looked away. "Well, it doesn't matter. I'll be here. You'll be there."

"What are you saying?"

Ashley stared at the lake as she tried to formulate her answer. Wouldn't it just be better to end their relationship now before...before he broke her heart? *Too late to keep that from happening.* Once he was back in Atlanta, he'd be easy to forget, wouldn't he? Or was she just kidding herself?

Finally, she looked up at him. "Since you're going back to Atlanta, there isn't much point to our dating anymore."

His handsome face bathed in moonlight, he stared back, his shoulders rigid. "Okay. If that's the way you want it."

"I do." Ashley watched him turn and walk away, her happiness going with him.

Chapter Sixteen

Papers and blueprints lay on Peter's desk in a neat arrangement. Everything was in perfect order except his love life. He had his dream job, but it didn't bring him the same happiness as working with Ashley and the mission project had. His office window gave him a perfect view of downtown Atlanta, but he longed for the views of the north Georgia mountains.

The weeks since Peter had taken the helm at Hiatt Construction had been hectic—each one filled with work that kept him so busy that he barely had time to contemplate Ashley's rejection. That was the good part.

The bad part was Richard's impending nuptials. Richard had asked Peter to be the best man, and the wedding was forcing him to confront his feelings for Ashley. How was he going to deal with seeing her again? He had a little more than twenty-four hours to figure that out.

Rather than tackling his feelings about the situation with Ashley, he'd buried himself in work. He couldn't hide behind that shield anymore. Finally, he had to admit he was miserable without her. He missed her laughter, the way she looked when she wrinkled her freckled nose and her penchant for speaking her mind. Most of all, he missed the way she challenged him to be a better person.

If giving up this job was what it took to convince her that he loved her, that's what he'd do. He'd spent years longing for this position, but without Ashley in his life, the job didn't fulfill any of his dreams.

While Peter's mind whirled with thoughts of Ashley, his assistant announced Richard's arrival. Peter hurried to greet Richard as he walked into the office. "Everything set for the big day?"

Richard nodded. "I just wanted to check in with you before I headed up north. I have a favor to ask."

"What's that?"

"Um…are you bringing a guest to the wedding?"

"You mean like a date?" Peter wondered where this was going. He hoped it didn't derail his plans for talking with Ashley.

"Yeah."

"No, I'm going by myself."

"Oh, good." Richard paused, seemingly embarrassed. "I hate to impose on you, but could you take Ashley under your wing? She's been up there in that little town all alone without a chance to find a date. I was hoping you could just make sure she's having a good time."

"No problem, sir. I'd be glad to do that. You can count on me."

"I knew I could. That's why you're my best man." Richard smiled.

"Does Ashley know you're asking me to do this?"

Richard grimaced. "No, she'd think I was trying to run her life. I just want to make sure she doesn't feel left out."

"I understand," Peter said, hoping Ashley didn't get wind of her father's request.

"Well, I'd better get going. See you tomorrow night."

Peter accompanied Richard to the door. "I'm looking forward to it."

With a renewed purpose, Peter formulated a strategy. When he went to the wedding, he had to do two things. First, he'd say he was sorry for abandoning the mission project. Then he'd tell Ashley how much he loved her and that he couldn't live without her. He had to convince her that they were right for each other—that they were meant to be together.

As Peter congratulated himself on his plan, his gaze fell on the Bible he kept on his desk. His heart sank. He'd forgotten one important thing. He'd left God out of his plan.

Plopping into the chair behind his desk, he bowed his head. *Lord, You know that I love Ashley and want to spend my life with her, but I'm turning my plan over to You.*

Ashley sat in the front row of chairs arranged on the yard of her father's lake-front home, waiting for the wedding to start. Ashley's heart sang with happiness for Charlotte and her dad. But a pall hung over her happiness much the same as the mist that hung over the mountains surrounding the lake, because she had to deal with Peter again today.

Last night at the rehearsal and dinner afterward, other than an initial greeting, she'd managed to avoid Peter. She doubted she could do that again today, especially during the reception.

Close family and friends gathered as music from a string quartet floated through the air. She didn't want to see Peter, his presence would only remind her of how she had pushed him away, but she'd put on a happy face for her father's sake.

The pastor took his place under the arbor covered with clematis vines, and Richard appeared with Peter at his side. She smiled at her dad but didn't dare meet Peter's gaze. Not that he was looking at her anyway.

The processional started with the little ring bearer, Charlotte's grandson, followed by her granddaughter as flower girl. Charlotte's daughter, Tammy, served as matron of honor.

Finally, escorted by her son, Ryan, Charlotte walked down the petal-strewn runner.

Tears welled in Ashley's eyes as she took in the happiness on her father's and Charlotte's faces as they said their vows. Ashley tried her best not to look at Peter, but she couldn't avoid it when he handed her dad the ring. Their gazes met, but she instantly looked away. Pressure filled her chest, as if a hand were squeezing her heart. She could hardly wait till this day was over.

Finally, the pastor pronounced Richard and Charlotte husband and wife. Her dad kissed his bride. The recessional played, and the bride and groom walked hand in hand down the aisle.

Ashley managed to endure the torturous photo session, where she had to be in several photos that included Peter. She smiled and pretended nothing was wrong. Surviving this day was a test of her fortitude.

The string quartet played while people mingled before the buffet dinner started. Ashley mingled, talking with Charlotte's family and several of her dad's business associates. She kept a careful eye out for Peter and made sure she was always on the opposite side of the room.

During dinner, guests were seated at tables set around the lower floor of the lake house, which opened onto the patio and yard beyond. After Ashley went through the buffet line, she found her place card at the wedding party's table. The real torture had begun. Peter's place was next to hers.

"Hello, Ashley. How have you been?" Peter asked, without even looking at her.

Miserable. Sitting, she put her plate on the table. "Fine. Is your new position everything you'd thought it would be?"

Still not looking her way, he picked up his fork and stabbed a piece of meat. "Yes. It's been a challenge. Your dad tells me you've taken over the mission project with great success. I knew you'd do a good job."

"Thanks."

Even Peter's kind words didn't prompt him to make eye contact. "Your dad also tells me you've rented your own place up here. Are you enjoying the quiet?"

Despite her melancholy, a smile tugged at her lips. "I like having my own place, but I actually miss the Weaver girls. So I've started a weekly Bible study with the teen girls from church."

Peter finally looked at her. "That sounds exactly like something you'd do. How's it going?"

"Good." Yeah, it was good for the teenaged girls, but Ashley's prayer life was suffering because she'd let this business with Peter fester. She'd actually started the study to try to rejuvenate her own spiritual life, but that wasn't going to happen until she made things right with Peter.

They fell silent as they continued to eat, and Ashley's thoughts went back to the night of her father's announcement and how she'd pushed Peter away. He'd never replied. He'd just walked away.

Somehow they'd managed to get through the remaining two weeks of the mission projects by staying out of each other's way. Ashley had barely acknowledged Peter's final day, when he cleaned out his desk and left. She regretted her attitude at his departure. She should ask for his forgiveness. She should get over her disappointment, but how could she when she still loved him? Seeing him today only made that more clear.

As the mealtime came to an end, Peter stood to give a toast. The room quieted. "I want to toast Richard and Charlotte. I've known them for over fifteen years, first as the boss and his housekeeper, then as friends. Richard has been more than a boss. He's been a mentor and like a second father to me. I want you to join me in wishing them years of happiness together."

Cheers and the clinking of glasses filled the room. Then Charlotte's daughter made her toast and had everyone laughing as she told how she finally convinced her mom it was okay to date her employer.

After she finished, Richard stood. "I want to thank everyone for coming and sharing our special day. And I want to especially thank Peter for being my best man. He says I'm like a second father to him. That warms my heart because he's like a son to me. He's been there whenever I've needed him."

Again the room filled with cheers, but tears filled Ashley's eyes. She blinked madly to hold them back. Now she saw what Peter meant when he said that her father needed him.

Her dad had depended on Peter for years, especially the years when she'd been gone. She hadn't been there for her dad, but Peter had. She'd been wrong to castigate Peter for taking her father's job offer. Sometime tonight she had to let him know. And she intended to lay her heart on the line by telling him she loved him.

She prayed he would accept her apology and her love.

Peter stood off to the side and watched Richard and Charlotte cut their cake. Being around Ashley was tearing him apart, because she was obviously trying to avoid him. He'd had little success in trying to talk with her, much less see that she was having a good time, as Richard had requested. How could he convince her that she needed him and his love?

The mission project and Ashley had made him examine his spiritual life, and he'd made a new commitment to God. Part of that commitment was a better prayer life. He'd prayed about his relationship with Ashley, and he'd felt God showing him that he could trust her not to break his heart. So what had gone wrong?

Peter didn't understand how God was working in this situation. Why did getting his dream job mean giving up his dream of sharing his life with Ashley? He'd tried to give the whole thing to God, but Peter constantly found himself trying to take it back. Had he made the wrong choice? He didn't know. He'd thrown himself into his new job in order to forget about Ashley, but that hadn't helped.

As Charlotte got ready to throw her bouquet, Tammy stepped beside him. "I have a feeling the bouquet is headed right for Ashley. Mom will see to it."

Peter tried to laugh. "But Ashley doesn't look too happy."

"I know. It's terrible to be one of the only single people at a wedding." Tammy got ready to take photos.

"Yeah." Was Tammy referring to him, too?

The bouquet flew through the air and landed at Ashley's feet. When she didn't immediately pick it up, Tammy rushed over. Laughing, she grabbed it and gave it to Ashley. "You know you were supposed to catch this."

"I know." As Ashley took the bouquet, her halfhearted smile tore at Peter's heart. She should be happy. She should be the next bride. She should be his bride. But she didn't want that. Could he change her mind?

Richard and Charlotte joined Ashley, and each of them gave her a hug. Charlotte said something Peter couldn't hear, but a pink tinge stained Ashley's cheeks. Charlotte said something else, and finally Ashley laughed. Her laughter wove its way through his brain and into his heart. He might survive the night, but he wasn't sure his heart would.

His stomach sank when he realized what came next—the garter toss. Did someone think up these wedding rituals to torture single people?

Before Peter could disappear, Ryan and Tammy pushed him out to the area where three other reluctant guys poked fun at each other while they waited for Richard to throw the garter. Richard grinned as he took off Charlotte's garter and looked directly at Peter. Okay. If Richard intended the garter for him, Peter was going after it.

And he was going after Ashley.

* * *

"Looks like Peter wants that garter." Tammy appeared at Ashley's side. "Does that have anything to do with the fact that you caught the bouquet?"

Ashley's heart hammered. Did it? Was it possible that she hadn't crushed every bit of his feelings for her? "He's just competitive. Besides, I didn't catch the bouquet. You gave it to me."

"That's because Mom's angling for you and Peter to get together." Tammy readied her camera.

Before Ashley could respond, her father flung the garter into the air. Peter grabbed it. Lots of backslapping and laughter followed. Her father shook Peter's hand, then glanced in her direction.

"Looks as though your dad's hoping for the same thing."

"It can't happen."

"Why not?"

Ashley released a harsh breath. "Because I messed up."

"Would you like to tell your new sister all about it?"

"Sister?"

"Well, stepsister, technically. But I've always wanted a sister."

"Me, too." Ashley smiled. "I never thought about you being my sister. That's cool. And yes, I'd love to tell my new sister what a mess I've made of things. That's what sisters are for, isn't it?"

"Absolutely."

"Let's get out of here, so we can talk."

After finding a quiet spot upstairs, Ashley had a heart-to-heart talk with Tammy. Ashley cried a little and laughed a little, then emerged from the room determined to plead her case to Peter. She hated to think of how much she'd hurt him because of her irrational fears. She'd been no better than the fiancée who'd run off with someone else.

Clutching the bridal bouquet, she went to find Peter. She spotted him heading toward the front of the house and followed.

When she got to the driveway, he disappeared behind her dad's car. She went to inspect.

She stepped behind the car. "What are you doing?"

A clattering noise sounded as he jumped up from his hunkered-down position. "Don't sneak up on a guy like that."

"Yes, sir." Her heart hammered. "What's going on here?"

He held up several ropes with old shoes and cans tied to the end. "It's the best man's job to put this stuff on the car."

"I see."

"Did you want something?"

"Yes. Your forgiveness."

Wrinkling his brow, he stared at her. "Did I hear you right?"

"Yes. I know I don't deserve it, but I'd like a second chance. You were right. Daddy needed you. Now I understand why you took the job. I saw that tonight when you gave the toast. Please forgive—"

Peter closed the distance between them and put a finger to her lips as he let the cans clang to the ground. "You talk too much."

He pulled her into his arms and kissed her. Her heart hammered for a whole different reason this time. When the kiss ended, she stayed wrapped in his arms and listened to his heart beat.

Finally, she looked up at him. "Does this mean you forgive me?"

He held her at arm's length. "Yes, but I'm the one who needs the forgiveness. I'm sorry I left the mission project after telling you that it was my new purpose in life."

"You shouldn't be sorry. Daddy needs you at Hiatt Construction. I was the selfish one, while you gave up everything to please my dad."

"You're giving me too much credit again." Peter smiled.

Ashley shook her head. "You deserve it."

"I don't know what I deserve, but there's one thing I want."

"What's that?"

"Your love. I love you, Ashley Hiatt. I've missed you. I can't seem to get along without you."

"You love me?"

"Yes, I do. More than I can explain."

"I love you, too." She held out the bouquet she still clutched in her hand. "Since I caught the bouquet and you caught the garter, will you marry me?"

Laughing, Peter pulled her back into his arms. "What should I do with a woman who speaks her mind?"

"Say yes."

"Yes."

"I love you so much." Ashley flung her arms around him. "Let's go tell Daddy."

* * * * *

Dear Reader,

As I was writing this story, I made a trip to the north Georgia mountains to refresh my memory of the area. Although I had visited before, while I lived in the Atlanta area in the 1980s, I enjoyed revisiting a place with some spectacular vistas that reminded me of God's wondrous creation. What a great God we have!

I hope you enjoyed this story of new beginnings for the heroine, Ashley, and a change of heart for the hero, Peter. When abrupt changes and turmoil occur in our lives, we may wonder why God has allowed such things to happen. We need to trust that God will guide our paths and lead us in a direction that will fulfill our calling. I hope you will seek God and his calling in your life.

I love to hear from readers. I enjoy your letters and e-mails so much. You can write to me at P.O. Box 16461, Fernandina Beach, Florida 32035, or through my Web site: www.merrilleewhren.com.

May God bless you,

Merrillee Whren

QUESTIONS FOR DISCUSSION

1. At the beginning of the story, Peter's boss asks him to pick up his daughter from the airport. Why do you suppose Peter isn't excited about the prospect? Has there ever been a time when you had to do something at work that didn't please you? If so, how did you handle the situation?

2. Why is Peter eager to please his boss? As Christians, how should we conduct ourselves in the workplace? What light does Colossians 3:23-24 shed on this subject?

3. Ashley has some preconceived ideas about the kind of person Peter is. On what does she base her opinion? What does she realize about her attitude toward Peter? Have you ever judged someone unfairly? What does 1 Samuel 16:7 tell us?

4. What has Ashley learned about material possessions while on the mission field? How are we supposed to view our earthly possessions? Read Matthew 6:19-20. What insight do you receive from these verses?

5. Ashley wonders why God allowed the unrest that required her to depart the mission field. Has there ever been a time when you had a plan to serve God, but it was derailed? How did you handle the situation? Did you find a new way to serve?

6. What were the consequences of Ashley's hurried shopping trip for clothes upon her arrival home? Have you ever suffered the consequences of a misguided decision?

7. Although Peter is Christian, he often puts his relationship

with God in second place behind his work. Even when he becomes part of the mission project, he is doing the work to please his boss rather than God. Has there ever been a time when you have put something before God? If so, how were you able to overcome this problem?

8. Peter sees in Ashley an example of someone who loves God and wants to serve Him. She makes Peter want to be a better person. Has there ever been someone in your life who has made you want to have a closer, more spiritual walk with God? If so, what did they do that prompted you to live a better life?

9. Why does meeting Libby and Jessica Weaver overwhelm Ashley? Has there ever been a time when you met someone who made you feel uncomfortable? If so, what was the reason? How did you deal with it?

10. Ashley and Peter have different views of life, so they must learn to work together by meshing their different styles. What can a person learn by working with someone who has a contrasting style? Do differing views help or hinder a project? Give a reason for your answer.

11. Peter has a dream of one day running Hiatt Construction, but as he takes the job of running the mission project, he sees that dream disappearing. Do you have a dream? Do you see the dream coming true? What part does God play in your dream? Read James 4:13-17.

12. Peter asks Ida to make cookies for the workers. What effect do you think the request has on Ida? Read Romans 12:6-8. What do these verses say about the way we help others?

13. Ashley and Peter enjoy different styles of worship. What style of worship do you enjoy? Why? What do Romans 12:1-3, John 4:22-24 and Colossians 2:16-17 say about worship?

14. What happened in Ashley's life that made her afraid to get too close to other people? How do you think this affects her relationship with Peter?

15. What happened in Peter's past that hurt him and made him reluctant to pursue his interest in Ashley? How can hurts from the past be overcome?

After weeks in intensive care, police officer Jude Sinclair is finally recovering from the hit-and-run accident that nearly cost him his life. But was it an accident after all? Jude has his doubts—which get stronger when he spots a familiar black car outside his house: the same kind that accelerated before running him down two months ago. Whoever wants him dead hasn't given up, and anyone close to Jude is in danger. Especially Lacey Carmichael, the stubborn, beautiful home-care aide who refuses to leave his side, even if it means following him into danger....

Probably heading for a back door.

"We don't have time for an argument," Jude said. "Take a look outside. What do you see?"

Lacey looked and shrugged. "The parking lot."

"Can you see your car?"

"Sure. It's parked under the streetlight. Why?"

"See the car to its left?"

"Yeah. It's a black sedan." Her heart skipped a beat as she said the words, and she leaned closer to the glass. "You don't think that's the same car you saw at the house tonight, do you?"

"I don't know, but I'm going to find out."

Lacey scooped up the grilled-cheese sandwich and shoved it into the carryout bag. "Let's go."

He eyed her for a moment, his jaw set, his gaze hot. *"We're* not going anywhere. You are staying here. I am going to talk to the driver of that car."

"I think we've been down this road before and I'm pretty sure we both know where it leads."

"It leads to you getting fired. Stay put until I get back, or forget about having a place of your own for a month." He stood and limped away, not even giving Lacey a second glance as he crossed the room and headed into the diner's kitchen area.

Probably heading for a back door.

Lacey gave him a one-minute head start and then followed, the hair on the back of her neck standing on end and issuing a warning she couldn't ignore. Danger. It was somewhere close by again, and there was no way she was going to let Jude walk into it alone. If he fired her, so be it. As a matter of fact, if he fired her, it might be for the best. Jude wasn't the kind of client she was used to working for. Sure, there'd been other young men, but none of them had seemed quite as vital or alive as Jude. He didn't seem to need her, and Lacey didn't want to be where she wasn't needed. On the other hand, she'd felt absolutely certain moving to Lynchburg was what God wanted her to do.

"So, which is it, Lord? Right or wrong?" She whispered the words as she slipped into the diner's hot kitchen. A cook glared at her, but she ignored him. Until she knew for sure why God had brought her to Lynchburg, Lacey could only do what she'd been paid to do—make sure Jude was okay.

With that in mind, she crossed the room, heading for the exit and the client that she was sure was going to be a lot more trouble than she'd anticipated when she'd accepted the job.

Jude eased around the corner of the restaurant, the dark alleyway offering him perfect cover as he peered into the parking lot. The car he'd spotted through the window of the restaurant was still parked beside Lacey's. Black. Four door. Honda. It matched the one that had pulled up in front of his house, and the one that had run him down in New York.

He needed to get closer.

A soft sound came from behind him. A rustle of fabric. A sigh of breath. Spring rain and wildflowers carried on the cold night air. Lacey.

Of course.

"I told you that you were going to be fired if you didn't stay where you were."

"Do you know how many times someone has threatened to fire me?"

"Based on what I've seen so far, a lot."

"Some of my clients fire me ten or twenty times a day."

"Then I guess I've got a ways to go." Jude reached back and grabbed her hand, pulling her up beside him.

"Is the car still there?"

"Yeah."

"Let me see." She squeezed in closer, her hair brushing his chin as she jockeyed for a better position.

Jude pulled her up short. Her wrist was warm beneath his hand. For a moment he was back in the restaurant, Lacey's creamy skin peeking out from under her dark sweater, white scars crisscrossing the tender flesh. She'd shoved her sleeve down too quickly for him to get a good look, but the glimpse he'd gotten was enough. There was a lot more to Lacey than met the eye. A lot she hid behind a quick smile and a quicker wit. She'd been hurt before, and he wouldn't let it happen again. No way was he going to drag her into danger. Not now. Not tomorrow. Not ever. As soon as they got back to the house, he was going to do exactly what he'd threatened—fire her.

"It's not the car." She said it with such authority, Jude stepped from the shadows and took a closer look.

"Why do you say that?"

"The one back at the house had tinted glass. Really dark. With this one, you can see in the back window. Looks like there is a couple sitting in the front seats. Unless you've got two people after you, I don't think that's the same car."

She was right.

Of course she was.

Jude could see inside the car, see the couple in the front seats. If he'd been thinking with his head instead of acting on the anger that had been simmering in his gut for months, he would have seen those things long before now. "You'd make a good detective, Lacey."

"You think so? Maybe I should make a career change. Give up home-care aide for something more dangerous and exciting." She laughed as she pulled away from his hold and stepped out into the parking lot, but there was tension in her shoulders and in the air. As if she sensed the danger that had been stalking Jude, felt it as clearly as Jude did.

"I'm not sure being a detective is as dangerous or as exciting as people think. Most days it's a lot of running into brick walls. Backing up, trying a new direction." He spoke as he led Lacey across the parking lot, his body still humming with adrenaline.

"That sounds like life to me. Running into brick walls, backing up and trying new directions."

"True, but in my job the brick walls happen every other day. In life, they're usually not as frequent." He waited while she got into her car, then closed the door, glancing in the black sedan as he walked past. An elderly woman smiled and waved at him, and Jude waved back, still irritated with himself for the mistake he'd made.

Now that he was closer, it was obvious the two cars he'd seen weren't the same. The one at his place had been sleeker and a little more sporty. Which proved that when a person wanted to see something badly enough, he did.

"That wasn't much of a meal for you. Sorry to cut things short for a false alarm." He glanced at Lacey as he got into the Mustang, and was surprised that her hand was shaking as she shoved the key into the ignition.

He put a hand on her forearm. "Are you okay?"

"Fine."

"For someone who is fine, your hands sure are shaking hard."

"How about we chalk it up to fatigue?"

"How about you admit you were scared?"

"Were? I still am." She started the car, and Jude let his hand fall away from her arm.

"You don't have to be. We're safe. For now."

"It's the 'for now' part that's got me worried. Who's trying to kill you, Jude? Why?"

"If I had the answers to those questions, we wouldn't be sitting here talking about it."

"You don't even have a suspect?"

"Lacey, I've got a dozen suspects. More. Every wife who's ever watched me cart her husband off to jail. Every son who's ever seen me put handcuffs on his dad. Every family member or friend who's sat through a murder trial and watched his loved one get convicted because of the evidence I put together."

"Have you made a list?"

"I've made a hundred lists. None of them has done me any good. Until the person responsible comes calling again, I've got no evidence, no clues and no way to link anyone to the hit and run."

"Maybe he won't come calling again. Maybe the hit and run was an accident, and maybe the sedan we saw outside your house was just someone who got lost and ended up in the wrong place." She sounded like she really wanted to believe it. He should let her. That's what he'd done with his family. Let them believe the hit and run was a fluke thing that had happened and was over. He'd done it to keep them safe. He'd do the opposite to keep Lacey from getting hurt.

* * * * *

*Will Jude manage to scare Lacey away,
or will he learn that the best way to keep her safe
is to keep her close...for as long as they both shall live?
To find out, read
THE DEFENDER'S DUTY
by Shirlee McCoy.
Available May 2009
from Love Inspired Suspense.*

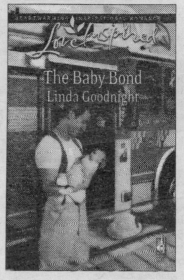

Love Inspired

Firefighter Nic Carano relishes his bachelor lifestyle. Then he loses his heart to a rescued baby. And when he meets the infant's lovely aunt, Nic starts considering love, marriage…and a baby carriage. But after all Cassidy Willis has been through, she's not convinced she wants to spend her life with someone whose life is always in danger.

Look for

The Baby Bond

by

Linda Goodnight

Available May wherever books are sold.

Love Inspired

TITLES AVAILABLE NEXT MONTH

Available April 28, 2009

BLIND-DATE BRIDE by Jillian Hart
The McKaslin Clan

It's police officer Max Decker's lucky day when he and
Brianna McKaslin both get stood up by their blind dates in
the same restaurant! Max isn't ready to give his heart to anyone,
especially someone as vulnerable as Brianna. But when he realizes
she's as sweet as the cakes she bakes, he's not sure he'll ever be able
to let her go.

THE BABY BOND by Linda Goodnight

Firefighter Nic Carano loves being a bachelor, until a rescued
baby leads him to the woman of his dreams. Suddenly a mother,
Cassidy Willis is grateful for all the help Nic and his family have
offered with her infant nephew, but she isn't sure she can give her
heart to someone whose life is always in danger. It's up to Nic
to show her the bond between them and her baby could be the
forever kind.

TIDES OF HOPE by Irene Hannon
Lighthouse Lane

Everyone in Nantucket may be smitten with Coast Guard
Lieutenant Craig Cole, but single mom Kate MacDonald can't
stand him, even if he has captured the heart of her little girl.
Kate doesn't want to like him—she certainly doesn't want to *love*
him—but Craig's quiet honor might win her heart after all.

THE COWBOY NEXT DOOR by Brenda Minton

Jay Blackhorse is not about to let a city girl like Lacey Gould get
under his skin. But that won't stop the cowboy cop from offering
her and her baby niece all the help he can. When a dark secret from
Lacey's past returns, will his help be enough? And who will help
Jay once he realizes he's fallen for the city girl next door?

LICNMBPA0409